KJELL ASKILDSEN

Everything Like Before

TRANSLATED FROM THE NORWEGIAN BY

Seán Kinsella

archipelago books

Library of Congress Cataloging-in-Publication Data
Names: Askildsen, Kjell, 1929- author. | Kinsella, Seán (Translator), translator.
Title: Everything like before / Kjell Askildsen ; translated from the Norwegian by Seán Kinsella.
Other titles: Alt som før. English
Description: First Archipelago Books edition. | Brooklyn, NY : Archipelago Books, 2021. |
First published as Alt som før by Forlaget Oktober.
Identifiers: LCCN 2020026811 (print) | LCCN 2020026812 (ebook) |
ISBN 9781939810946 (trade paperback) | ISBN 9781939810953 (ebook)
Classification: LCC PT8950.A769 A2 2021 (print) | LCC PT8950.A769 (ebook) | DDC 839.823/74—dc23
LC record available at https://lccn.loc.gov/2020026811
LC ebook record available at https://lccn.loc.gov/2020026812

Archipelago Books
232 3rd Street #A111
Brooklyn, NY 11215
www.archipelagobooks.org

Distributed by Penguin Random House
www.penguinrandomhouse.com

Cover art by Nikolai Astrup

This translation has been published with the financial support of NORLA.
This publication was made possible with support from the Lannan Foundation,
the New York State Council on the Arts, a state agency, the New York City Department
of Cultural Affairs, and the Carl Lesnor Family Foundation.

PRINTED IN THE UNITED STATES OF AMERICA

Contents

EVERYTHING LIKE BEFORE

A Bucket of Time

IT WAS EITHER in October or November; I ought to remember if the leaves had fallen, there's something reassuring about specifying a precise time, for how can I rely on that part of my memory dictating the event itself when I've forgotten important details of the setting, one thing being so dependent on other things after all, and time is part of the setting.

I spotted him as I emerged from the woods and was about to cross the road. I ran back into the woods. He was coming from the city and was on the way home. He was carrying the bucket in his hand – a bucket of time you might say – and I lay quite still behind a stone, hearing the alarm clock tick. He was a big man and moved heavily; he was wearing an old, ankle-length coat; I imagined I knew his smell but that was most likely a delusion influenced by my secondhand knowledge of his miserable existence.

I followed him, at a safe distance – I knew where he was headed after all. I acted in accordance with my nature, my voyeuristic disposition: I've experienced little in my life but seen a great deal, in other words my experiences are for all intents and purposes secondhand. So I followed him, but pretended – also to myself – as though it simply came about, that I happened to be going the same way. It's important not to set one's goals too clearly, so as to safeguard oneself against failure. I watched him leave the road and make his way across the field along the stream; I myself walked along the edge of the woods, hidden by the willow scrub so he couldn't see me. I believe that a man walking that way – alone on his way home from the city – is thinking about the past, that he's sad yet relieved to have put people behind him, above all children, because you can't walk around with an alarm clock in a milk pail with impunity, whoever does that must either be full of forbearance or full of contempt. I believe he was thinking about the past, perhaps – it being an autumn day – about having lived so long only to be so lonely. I remember now that it must have been in November, otherwise I wouldn't have wondered what kind of Christmas a man like that would have; I was child enough to measure a man's loneliness by how he spent Christmas Day – you can see by that how time enters into it.

He lived in one corner of a dilapidated outlying barn enclosed by forest on all sides. He went inside but emerged immediately afterward and sat down on a stool. There wasn't much to look at, he just sat there, with his elbows on his knees; I was thinking he was old enough to stay sitting there until the sun went down, and I felt he must be the loneliest person on earth. So really not much to look at – an old man on a stool – and I was about to leave when he moved. He took something from his inside pocket: a whistle. He put it to his lips and blew the hymn *Nu*

Titte til hinanden – it was very beautiful, a morning song in an evening wood, played by an old man on a stool in front of a ramshackle barn.

He played the tune twice, then put the whistle in his pocket and stood up. He gazed between the tree trunks, a long searching look, as though to assure himself he was alone. Then he began to speak, slowly and distinctly, as though the trees were hard of hearing. It was the kind of speech you make in private, words from the top of your head, seemingly absurd digressions spun off tenuously connected themes; if I hadn't used nature as an auditorium for similar speeches myself, I'd probably have thought he'd lost his mind, but I knew better. He stood putting himself to rights after his trip to the city; he spoke about stares as long as church steeples and made his tormentors out to be rats and a brood of vipers; he was vague but eloquent – it was a wonderful performance, played out as the sun set behind the silent forest, and when he stopped there fell a hush, as though after a mournful song.

The silence was suddenly broken by a round of applause, and from out of the woods emerged two young men, the sons of Ellerman, the tinsmith. They continued to clap as they approached the old man, who stood motionless beside the stool. They came to a halt in front of him.

"So, you squeak, do you?"

He made no answer.

"Sit down."

He remained standing. They pushed him onto the stool.

"What are we to do with an idiot like this?"

"He squeaked, didn't he?"

One of them put his hand inside the old man's coat and pulled out the whistle. He held it between two fingers and said something I couldn't make out. The old man let out a yell and tried to grab it from him. That was ill-advised, his resistance provoked them. I saw the whistle fly in an arc through the air, landing a few meters away from me; it sounded like it struck a stone. I was angry but didn't allow myself to be lured, my anger was in check, as always; cowardice often prevents one from acting rashly; it's no coincidence that cowardly people are often credited with high intelligence. So I did nothing, but allowed developments run their course independent of my disgust. I did not hear everything they said but saw all the more for that. One of the brothers went into the barn and appeared again with the milk pail. He was holding his nose.

"Gosh, dat was a glose gall!"

The other brother laughed. They lifted the lid off the bucket and bent over it. The old man cried out and stood up but they paid him no attention. It was an old-fashioned alarm clock, almost as big as the lid of the bucket. They talked and pointed skyward.

"No!" the old man yelled. "You don't know what you're doing!"

They glanced at him, and I think they almost thought better of it; I'm willing to credit them with some hesitation, a moment's indecision, before prestige got the upper hand.

"Do you reckon this is his heart?"

"Sounds like it. What do you think it looks like?"

"We'll see."

They began picking the alarm clock apart, talking and laughing, and dropping the loose parts into the bucket. The old man stood a few steps away, silent and motionless. The sun was gone; it was so quiet I could hear the screws ring against the bottom of the bucket. Then it was over.

"That wasn't much of a heart."

The old man didn't move; he stood like a statue – as if time had really come to an end, as if his heart lay at the bottom of the pail, broken.

The brothers seemed oddly harmless after finishing their deed. They tried to drag out their easy victory with taunts, but it was no use, the victory was slipping from their grasp, leaving only losers: the old man, the brothers, me, and a forest full of defeat. Then they withdrew among the tree trunks, without rounds of applause but with jarring laughter.

The voices faded, dusk fell. I emerged from my hiding place and began looking for the whistle. He saw me no doubt but he didn't move. The whistle wasn't hard to find. I picked it up and approached him, I, the brothers' counterpart, an outstretched hand.

"It's in one piece."

He took it without a word and without looking at it. I'd never been so close to him before; time had plowed deep furrows in his face. I couldn't think of anything to say. His big eyes rested on me. It was uncomfortable; I had let my emotions get the better of me and broken the voyeur's first commandment: never be seen. He saw, and perhaps I gave him a little comfort, because he must surely have despised me.

But he didn't say a word, and after a moment he bent down, grabbed the bucket and headed for the door.

I entered the forest where the trees grew most densely, walking slowly, so he wouldn't see that I was ashamed. But I doubt he was thinking about me, because I hadn't taken many steps before an awful din broke out in the ramshackle barn, a racket so loud it sounded like everything behind those four walls was being smashed to pieces. The whistle too, perhaps.

A Lovely Spot

"AREN'T YOU DRIVING a little fast?" she said.

"No," he said.

A little while later he turned off the motorway and onto the narrow winding road towards the fjord.

"It's so green since we were last here."

"Yes," he said.

"It's as if the road is narrower," she said.

"I'm not driving too fast," he said.

Just before they got to the big oak tree where he usually left the car, she said she had a feeling that something wasn't quite right. She usually said that when they were drawing close to the summerhouse, and he didn't reply. One time she may be right, he thought.

He parked the car. He helped her with the lightest backpack.

"Just start walking," he said.

"I'll wait for you," she said.

"I'll catch up," he said.

He caught up with her halfway down the steep, overgrown dirt road. She was standing waiting for him.

"Is it heavy?" he said.

"No," she said.

They walked on. After a few minutes the house came into view below them. He slowed down; she always walked in front for the last few meters. She opened the gate, then she said:

"Somebody's been here."

"Oh?" he said.

"I left a stone on the gatepost," she said, "and now it's gone."

"Well," he said, "I guess somebody's taken it. Was there something special about it?"

"No," she said, "an ordinary stone."

He closed the gate after himself.

"I don't like the fact someone's been here," she said.

He did not reply. He saw that the apple tree was in bloom.

"Look at the apple tree," he said.

"Yes," she said, "isn't it beautiful."

She reached the door. She took off the backpack. He walked over to her, placed the shopping bags beside her backpack and took the key from his pocket.

"Do you want to open it?" he asked.

"You do it," she said.

He opened the door and went inside. He put down his backpack on the kitchen floor and continued into the living room. He opened a window and stood looking out over the fjord. She called to him. He went out to her.

"Would you be a dear and hoist the flag," she said.

"Now?" he said.

"I like people to see that we're here."

He looked at her, then picked up the shopping bags and went back inside. He fetched the flag from the drawer of the dresser in the hall.

"It was always the first thing Dad did," she said, "hoist the flag."

"Yes," he said, "I'm aware of that."

"You don't mind, do you?"

"I just got it, didn't I," he said.

He went over to the flagpole.

They were by the kitchen table. They had eaten. She sat looking out the window, in the direction of the dense forest.

"Isn't this a lovely spot," she said.

"Certainly is," he said.

"I don't think there's anyone who has a nicer place," she said.

He did not reply.

"I just wish we could cut back all that scrub at the edge of the forest."

"Why?" he said.

"It's just so . . . you can't see what's behind it."

"It's not on our property," he said.

"No," she said, "but still. Dad used to always cut it back."

They sat in silence for a while.

"What will we do tomorrow?" she said.

"Are we going to do something?" he said.

"No, I don't know," she said. "Take the rowboat out. To Ormøya, for example."

"It's nice just being here," he said.

"Of course. Yes, we'll stay put then, will we? Besides we've got plenty to do here."

"We're going to take it easy tomorrow," he said.

"But the outside toilet needs to be emptied," she said.

"There's no hurry," he said.

"No, just as long as it gets done."

They stood on the concrete jetty, the sun was about to set.

"Oh, how I love this place," she said.

He did not say anything.

"There. I fell into the sea right there."

"Yes," he said, "you've told me."

"I must have been about four years old," she said.

"Five," he said.

"Yes, maybe. I struck my head against one of the stones you can see there and it left a deep cut above my ear, and if Dad hadn't – What was that?"

"It sounded like an animal," he said.

"It was someone shouting," she said.

"No, it sounded more like an animal."

"Let's go inside," she said.

They walked towards the house.

"We have to remember to take down the flag," she said.

"It's not necessary," he said.

"We've always done it," she said.

"Yes," he said, "I know."

"There's a rule requiring you to," she said.

"I know," he said.

"I want you to do it, Martin. If not, I'll do it myself."

"All right, all right, I'll do it."

When he came in, he said:

"I'm opening a bottle of wine."

"Yes, do that," she said.

She sat down on the bench. He poured wine in her glass.

"Thanks, that's enough," she said.

He poured himself twice as much and sat down by the window.

"That's where Dad used to sit," she said.

"Yes, you've told me," he said. "And where did your mother usually sit?"

"Mom? She . . . Why do you ask?"

"I was just wondering. Cheers."

"I think she normally sat here on the bench."

She sipped at her wine. They sat in silence. He pushed his chair back a little so he could look out at the fjord without having to turn his head. He drank.

"It's so quiet," she said.

He did not reply. Then he said:

"There's a man standing over there on the headland."

She got up and went to the window.

"He's looking this way," she said.

She opened the window.

"Why are you opening the window?" he said.

"So he'll see that there's somebody here."

"Why?" he said.

"So he'll keep away. You see, now he's gone."

She closed the window and went to sit down.

He looked at her.

"Why are you looking at me like that?" she said.

"I'm just looking at you," he said. "Cheers."

He drained the glass, got up, went over to the table and poured more wine in it.

"Have you locked the door?" she said.

"No," he said.

"Could you do it?" she said.

"When we're going to bed," he said. "We never lock it before we go to bed."

"Just this once," she said.

"Why?"

She did not reply. He went out into the hall. He opened the door and looked towards the gate and the forest, then he closed and locked it. He stood a few moments in the half-light of the hall, all he could hear was his own breath.

"Martin," she said.

He went into her.

"I thought you'd gone out," she said.

He did not reply. He took a gulp from his glass. She checked the time.

"I think I'll go to bed soon," she said.

"Yeah, do that," he said.

"Are you going to bed?" she asked.

"Not just yet. It's nice to sit looking out at the fjord."

"Yes, isn't it?" she said. "Isn't it a lovely spot?"

"Certainly is," he said.

He looked at her.

"I think you're looking at me so strangely," she said.

"You think?" he said.

She took hold of her glass. She drank up.

"I'm sorry I'm so tired," she said. "It's probably all the fresh air."

"Yes," he said. "Just go on to bed."

She was asleep. He undressed and crept under the duvet. She was lying with her back to him. After a while he placed his hand on her hip. She gave a low moan. He left his hand there. He felt his member grow. He moved his hand a little further down. Her body gave a start, as though from an electric shock. He withdrew his hand and turned the other way.

He had been up to the car to fetch a coil of rope. On the way back he stopped by the gate and stood surveying the house and property. Then he picked up a stone and put it on the gatepost. He walked down around the front of the house and over to the boathouse. She was lying on the jetty reading. He hung the rope on a peg under the eave, then sat down with his back to the wall and looked out over the fjord.

After a few minutes he went over to her. She looked up and smiled.

"Isn't it lovely?" she said.

"Isn't what lovely?" he said.

"Lovely here," she said.

"Certainly is," he said.

"Why don't you fetch the other mattress and lie down here in the sun," she said.

He did not reply. He looked up at the house and said:

"The swallows haven't arrived yet."

"They could be here any time," she said. "It's around about now that they come."

"If they come," he said.

"I'm sure they will. They always have. Once, Dad saw them as they arrived. They flew straight in under the same roof tile as the year before."

"Yes, you told me that."

"In the old days people believed that a swallow building its nest in a house meant good luck for the people living there."

"Yes," he said.

He started walking up towards the house.

He had carried a deckchair over to the apple tree and was lying back in it and looking up towards the forest. Suddenly, he heard her call his name, loudly, as if something had happened. He got up and walked down towards the jetty. She was sitting upright, her back to the fjord.

"What is it?" he said.

She waved him closer.

"He was there again, that man, on the headland."

"So what?" he said.

"I called out to you so he'd realize that I wasn't on my own."

He looked at her.

"Are you afraid that he's going to come and get you?" he said.

"Oh Martin. Really," she said.

He continued to look at her, before turning and walking towards the back of the house.

They had eaten. A bank of clouds had built up in the west and the low sun had disappeared behind it. She was sitting on the bench, reading; he was standing by the window looking out over the fjord.

"I'll open a bottle of wine," he said.

"Yes," she said, "do that."

He uncorked the bottle and placed it on the table in front of her, along with two glasses. He filled her glass right up.

"That's a lot!" she said.

"Yes," he said.

He took his own glass and sat down in the chair by the window.

"You seem to like sitting there," she said.

"Yes," he said.

She continued reading. After a while she looked up and said:

"Have you lowered the flag?"

"Yes," he said.

"Have you?" she said.

"No," he said.

"Why did you say yes?" she said.

He did not reply. Then he said:

"I'm going into town tomorrow to buy a pennant."

"Oh no," she said, "not a pennant, they're so . . . we've never had a pennant."

He didn't reply.

She put down her book, got up and went into the kitchen. He heard her open and close the front door, then it was quiet. He took a gulp of wine, then another. He walked over to the table and filled his glass. He sat down and looked out over the fjord. After a while the door opened. He heard her pull out the drawer in the dresser, then push it in again. She came into the living room and sat down on the bench.

"Cheers," she said.

"Cheers," he said.

They drank.

"I took down the flag," she said. "I'm sorry if it seems like I think you should be the one to do it."

He did not reply.

"It's just that you always do it," she said. "I didn't know you minded."

He did not reply.

"You know," she said, "I've never done it before. It was always Dad who did it. And then you. I've never been here on my own."

"No, I know," he said.

They had been sitting in silence for a long time. She was reading. He had finished his wine and refilled his glass. She put the book aside.

"I think I'm getting tired," she said. "What time is it?"

"Ten past ten," he said.

"Well, no wonder," she said. "I was up so early."

"I'm going to turn in as well," he said.

"I don't mind if you stay up," she said.

She got to her feet.

"Okay," he said. "Then I might as well stay up for a little while."

"After all," she said, "you've still got half a glass of wine left."

"Yes, I can see that," he said.

When it had grown quiet in the house, he put on a windbreaker and went out the front door. He stood on the jetty for a while, then began making his way over toward the headland. There was a pale crescent moon above the hill in the east. The air was still, and the sea gurgled almost soundlessly between the rocks by the shore.

He stood for a few minutes at the tip of the headland, then he walked quickly back to the house and in the front door. He opened another bottle of wine and sat down on the bench. It was past eleven o'clock. An hour later the bottle was empty. He put the two empty bottles beside each other on the table and stood up. He took off the windbreaker and threw it on the bench. He walked through the kitchen and up the stairs, opened the door to the bedroom and switched on the light. She was lying with her back to him. She did not move. He went over to the closet and took out a woollen blanket. Mothballs fell down onto the floor. He slammed the closet door. She did not stir. He tugged the duvet off her.

"Martin!" she said.

"Just lie there!" he said.

"What is it?" she said.

"Just lie there!" he said.

Then he left.

She was lying on the jetty. He saw her through the living room window. The wine bottles and glasses had been cleared away. The windbreaker lay on the bench.

He went outside and walked to the gate. He picked up the stone on the gatepost and flung it away, then he continued on up the dirt road.

He got into the car and started the engine. He backed the car out onto the road, then he reversed in again and turned off the engine. He sat quite still looking straight ahead for a long time.

He met her on his way back down to the house.

"Where have you been?" she said.

"Just for a walk," he said.

"You could have told me," she said. "I couldn't find you anywhere."

"I just went for a walk," he said.

"I was scared," she said.

"Why?" he said.

"You know why," she said. "Last night, and now this."

"Forget about last night," he said.

She looked at him.

"Forget about it," he said. "I'd had too much to drink, it was nothing, I don't know what it was."

"I was beside myself," she said.

"Were you?" he said.

He began to walk down towards the house. She followed after.

He sat at the end of the jetty looking out over the fjord. She was lying behind him, sunning herself. She said:

"Isn't it a lovely spot."

"Certainly is," he said.

A Sudden Liberating Thought

I LIVE IN a basement; a result of having come down in the world, in every sense.

My room has only one window, and only the upper part of it is above pavement level; causing me to see the world outside from below. It's not a very big world, but it often feels big enough.

I see only the legs and lower parts of the passersby on the pavement on my side of the street, but having lived here for four years, I can tell whom they belong to in most cases. That's due to there being little traffic; I live almost at the end of a cul-de-sac.

I'm a taciturn man, but I talk to myself on occasion. The things I say at those times have to be said, I think.

One day while I was standing by the window, and had just seen the lower part of the landlord's wife go past, I suddenly felt so lonely that I decided to go out.

I put on my shoes and coat, and stuck my reading glasses in my coat pocket, just in case. Then I went out. The advantage of living in a basement is that you walk up the steps when you're rested and down them when you come home tired. It's probably the only advantage.

It was a warm summer's day. I walked to the park by the disused fire station, where I can usually sit in peace. But I'd hardly sat down when an old chap my own age came along and parked himself beside me, even though there were plenty of unoccupied benches. I *had* gone out because I was feeling lonely, but not to talk, just for a change. I began to grow increasingly nervous that he would say something, so much so I considered getting up and walking off, but where would I go, after all this was where I'd planned on coming. But he didn't say anything, and I found that so appealing I became favorably disposed towards him. I even tried to look at him, without him noticing of course. But he did notice, because he said:

"Forgive me for saying, but I sat here because I thought I'd be left in peace. I can move, of course, if you'd like."

"Sit, by all means," I said, more than a little taken aback. Naturally I made no further attempts to look at him, he had my deepest respect. And more naturally still, I did not speak to him. I felt a little strange inside, somewhat non-lonely, a wellbeing of sorts.

He sat there for a half hour, then rose to his feet, with a little difficulty, turned to me and said:

"Thank you. Goodbye."

"Goodbye."

Then he left, with a remarkably long stride and slightly flailing arms, as though sleepwalking.

The following day at the same time, or rather, a little earlier, I walked to the park again. In light of all the thought and speculation he had caused me, it seemed the natural course of action; it was hardly a free choice, whatever that is.

He came, I spotted him from some way off, recognizing him by his gait. There were unoccupied benches that day too and I was intrigued to see if he would sit down beside me. I looked in the other direction of course, acting as though I hadn't seen him, and when he sat down, I pretended not to notice. He made no sign of registering my presence either; it was a rather unusual situation – a sort of unplanned non-meeting. I have to admit I was uncertain whether or not I wanted him to say something, and after a half hour I was just as uncertain about whether I should leave first or wait for him to go. Not that this uncertainty bothered me that much – I could have remained sitting in any case. But then for some reason or other I got it into my head that he had the upper hand and that made the decision easy. I stood up, looked at him for the first time and said:

"Goodbye."

"Goodbye," he replied, looking me squarely in the eyes. His gaze was unflinching.

I left, and as I walked away I couldn't help but wonder how he would characterize *my* gait, and immediately felt my body tense up and my steps become stiff and awkward. I have to admit, it annoyed me.

That evening, as I stood beneath the window looking out – there wasn't much too see – I decided that if he came the next day I'd say something. I even planned on what to say, how to initiate what could potentially become a conversation. I would wait a quarter of an hour, then, without looking at him, I'd say: "It's time we spoke." No more, just that. He could either reply or not, and if he didn't reply I would stand up and say: "In the future I'd prefer it if you found another bench to sit on."

I also came up with a lot of other things that evening, things to say if a conversation developed, but I rejected most of them as uninteresting or too trite.

The next morning I was excited and uncertain, I even considered staying home. I resolved to dismiss the decision I'd come to the previous evening; if I went there, I was definitely not going to say anything.

I went, and he came. I didn't look at him. It suddenly occurred to me as rather striking that he always showed up within five minutes of my arriving – as though he'd been standing somewhere nearby and seen me come. Of course, I thought, of course: he lives in one of the buildings beside the fire station and sees me from his window.

I didn't have time to speculate any further because he suddenly began to speak. His words made me feel somewhat ill at ease I have to admit.

"Excuse me," he said, "but if you don't mind, perhaps it's time we spoke together."

I made no immediate reply, but after a few moments I said:

"Perhaps. If there's anything to say."

"You don't know if there's anything to say?"

"I'm probably older than you."

"It's not impossible."

I didn't say any more. I felt an unpleasant uneasiness within, which had to do with the odd role reversal that had taken place. He'd been the one to initiate the conversation, using almost my own words, and I was the one who replied as I'd imagined him doing. It was as though I could just as well be him and he could just as well be me. It was unpleasant. I felt like leaving. But seeing as I had been, so to speak, forced to identify with him, I found it hard to hurt or even insult him.

Perhaps a minute passed, then he said:

"I'm eighty-three."

"Then I was right."

Another minute went by.

"Do you play chess?" he asked.

"It's been a long time."

"Hardly anyone plays chess anymore. Everyone I've played chess with is dead."

"At least fifteen years ago."

"The last one died in the winter. No great loss actually, he had become rather dull-witted. I always beat him in less than twenty moves. But he got a certain pleasure out of it, his one remaining pleasure in life I dare say. Perhaps you knew him."

"No," I quickly replied, "I didn't know him."

"But how can you be so sure that . . . well, that's your business."

He was right about that and I would have told him as much, but to his credit he hadn't completed the question.

I noticed he turned his face to look at me. He sat like that for a good while; it was unpleasant, so I took my glasses from my coat pocket and put them on. Everything in front of me – the trees, houses, benches – all disappeared into a haze.

"You're short-sighted?" he asked after a while.

"No," I said, "quite the opposite."

"What I mean is, you need glasses to see what's far away."

"No, on the contrary. It's things that are close to me that I have problems with."

"I see."

I didn't say any more. When I noticed him turning his face away again I removed my glasses and put them in my coat pocket. He didn't say any more either, so when I thought enough time had passed I stood up and politely said:

"Thanks for the chat. So long."

"So long."

I left with more confidence in my step that day, but on making it home and calming down, I began once again to hastily plan my next meeting with him. I paced back and forth thinking up many absurdities, a few subtleties too; I wasn't above exulting a little, but that, after all, was because I regarded him as my equal.

I didn't sleep well that night. Back when I was still young enough to believe the future could hold surprises in store I often slept poorly, but that was a long time ago, before it became clear to me, I mean completely clear, that the day you die, it makes no difference whether you've had a good life or a bad one. So the fact I slept poorly that night both surprised and unsettled me. Nor had I eaten anything to cause it either, only a few boiled potatoes and a tin of sardines; I'd had an excellent night's sleep many times before after such a meal.

The following day he didn't arrive until almost a quarter of an hour had passed. I'd begun to give up hope, a feeling I was unaccustomed to: having a hope to give up. But he came.

"Hello," he said.

"Hello."

We didn't say anything else for a while. I knew well what I was going to say if the silence went on too long, but I wanted him to speak first, and he did:

"Your wife . . . is she still alive?"

"No, she's not, died a long time ago, I've all but forgotten her. And your own?"

"Passed away two years ago. Today."

"Oh. So it's a day of mourning of sorts."

"Well. The feeling of loss, there's nothing you can do about that really. But I don't mark it by going to her grave, if that's what you mean. Graves are damnable places. Pardon me. That wasn't a very good choice of words."

I made no reply.

"My apologies," he said, "perhaps I've offended you, it wasn't my intention."

"You haven't offended me."

"Good. You might be religious for all I know. I had a sister who believed in eternal life. Such conceit."

Again I was struck by how he sat there delivering my line, and for a moment I was foolish enough to think that I was imagining everything, that he didn't even exist, and that in reality I was sitting talking to myself. And I suppose it was this foolishness that prompted me to pose a completely ill-considered question:

"Who are you really?"

Fortunately he didn't answer straight away, so I managed to retrieve the situation somewhat:

"Don't get me wrong. I wasn't actually talking to you. It was just something that came to mind."

I noticed he was looking at me, but this time I didn't take out my glasses. I said:

"Besides I wouldn't like you to think I'm in the habit of asking questions about which there are no answers."

Then we sat in silence. It wasn't a relaxing silence; I was tempted to leave. Two minutes, I thought, if he hasn't said anything by then, I'll go. I began counting the seconds in my head. He didn't say anything and after exactly two minutes I got to my feet. He stood up as well, at the very same time.

"Thanks for the chat," I said.

"Likewise. A shame you won't play chess."

"I don't think you'd enjoy it much. Besides, your opponents have a tendency to die."

"True, true," he replied, seeming suddenly abstracted.

"So long," I said.

"So long."

I was more tired than usual when I arrived home; I had to lie down on the bed. After a while I said aloud: "I'm old. And life is long."

When I woke up the next day it was raining. To say I was disappointed would be an understatement. But as the day wore on and the rain didn't let up it became clear to me that I would go to the park regardless. I couldn't do otherwise. It wasn't about him also turning up, that wasn't it. It was just that if he did come, then I wanted, I *had*, to be there. And as I was sitting there on that wet bench, in the rain, I even hoped he wouldn't show; there was something revealing, something brazen, about sitting completely alone in a rain-soaked park.

But he did come – as I knew he would! Unlike me he was wearing a raincoat, a long, black one reaching almost to the ground. He sat down.

"You braved the elements," he said.

It was of course only meant as a casual comment, but in light of what

I'd been thinking just prior to his turning up I found it rather impertinent, so I didn't reply. I noticed I was in bad humor and regretted having come. Moreover I was getting wet, my coat felt heavy, and to remain sitting seemed almost ludicrous, so I said:

"I came outside to get some fresh air, but then I got tired. I am an old man."

And to dispel any notions he might have, I added:

"A habit of mine, you understand."

He didn't say anything and it had the effect, albeit unreasonable, of provoking me. And what he eventually said, after a long pause, didn't serve to soften my attitude.

"You don't like people very much, do you, or am I mistaken?"

"Like people?" I replied. "What do you mean by that?"

"Well, it's just the kind of thing one says, isn't it? I didn't mean to be intrusive."

"Of course I don't like people. And of course I like people. Had you asked if I liked cats or goats, or butterflies for that matter, but people. Besides, I hardly know any."

I immediately regretted the last part, but fortunately that wasn't what he seized upon.

"Well, I never!" he said. "Goats and butterflies!"

I could tell he was smiling. I had to admit I'd been unnecessarily dismissive, so I said:

"If you want a general answer to a general question, then I like both goats and butterflies more unconditionally than I like people."

"Thank you, I got the point a while back. I'll remember to be more specific the next time I venture to ask something."

He said this in a friendly tone and it was no exaggeration to say I was sorry, even though my being difficult was down to the bad humor I was in. And because I was sorry, I said something I also immediately felt sorry for having said:

"Apologies, but words are nearly all I have left. I do apologize."

"Heavens, no. It was my fault. I should have taken into account who you are."

I felt my heart drop – did he know who I was? Did he come here every day because he knew who I was? I couldn't help feeling nervous and uncertain, and automatically put my hand in my coat pocket to get my glasses.

"What do you mean?" I said. "Do you know me?"

"Yes. I suppose you could say that. We have met before. I wasn't aware of that when I sat down here the first time. It gradually dawned on me that I'd seen you before, but I couldn't manage to place you, not until yesterday. It was something you said, and suddenly I realized where I knew you from. But you don't remember me?"

I got to my feet.

"No."

I looked directly at him. I didn't know if I'd ever seen him before.

"I am . . . I was your judge."

"You, you . . ."

I didn't know what else to say.

"Sit down, please."

"I'm wet. So, you were . . . that was you. I see. Well, goodbye, I have to go."

I left. It was no dignified exit, but I was unnerved, and walked faster than I had in years. When I got home I just about managed to pull my soaked overcoat off me before I collapsed onto the bed. My heart was pounding and I resolved never to return to the park.

But after a while, my heart rate returned to normal, as did my thoughts. I accepted my reaction, something hidden had come to light again, and I'd been caught off guard, that was all. It was understandable.

I got up from the bed and I could, not without some satisfaction, state that I was back to my old self again. I stood under the window and said aloud: "He'll see me again."

The fine weather made a return the following day, which was a relief, and my coat was as good as dry. I left for the park at the usual time; he wasn't going to notice anything out of the ordinary with me that might make him think he'd gained the upper hand.

But as I approached the bench I saw he was already there, hence he was the one acting out of the ordinary.

"Hello," he said.

"Hello," I replied as I sat down, and in order to take the bull by the horns I immediately added:

"I thought you might not show up today."

"Bravo," he said. "One nil to you."

I was content with that answer; he was an equal.

"Did you often feel guilty?" I asked.

"I don't follow."

"As a judge, did you often feel guilty? After all it was your occupation to assign to others the requisite amount of guilt."

"My occupation was to define the law based upon other people's assessment of guilt."

"Are you trying to excuse yourself? There's no need."

"I didn't feel guilty. I did, on the other hand, often feel at the mercy of the rigid nature of the law. As in your case."

"Yes, because you're not superstitious, after all."

He glanced at me.

"What does that mean?" he asked.

"Only superstitious people believe it's a doctor's obligation to prolong the suffering of those who are doomed."

"Ah, I understand. But aren't you afraid that the legalization of euthanasia could be misused?"

"Of course it couldn't be misused. Because then euthanasia would no longer be euthanasia but murder."

He made no reply. I snatched a sidelong glance at him; he had a sullen, impassive expression. That was fine by me. Although I didn't know whether his sullenness was due to what I'd said or if he was simply in the habit of looking like that, it was hard to tell, seeing as I'd practically never looked at him. Now I felt like making up for lost time and taking a good look at him, and I did, openly, turning my head to stare at his profile; it was the least I could permit myself when faced with the man who had sentenced me to several years in prison. I even took my glasses from my coat pocket and put them on; not that it was necessary, I could see him quite clearly without them, but I felt a sudden urge to provoke him. It was so unlike me to stare so overtly at a person that for a moment I felt like a stranger to myself; it was an odd and by no means unpleasant sensation. And breaking with my usual behavior in this way had a knock-on effect. I laughed for the first time in years; it doubtless sounded nasty. Without looking at me, he said in a brusque tone:

"I don't care what you're laughing at but it doesn't sound like you're enjoying yourself. And that's a pity. In other respects you're a sensible person."

His words disarmed me, as well as making me feel slightly ashamed, and I looked away from his angry profile and said:

"You're right. It wasn't much of a laugh."

I wasn't going to give him more than that.

We sat in silence; I thought about my miserable life and grew gloomy. I pictured the judge's home, with good chairs and large bookshelves.

"You probably have a housekeeper?" I said.

"Yes. Why do you ask?"

"I'm just trying to imagine what retirement looks like for a judge."

"Oh, it's nothing to brag about. The inactivity, you know, the long aimless days."

"Yes, time won't pass."

"And it's the only thing left."

"Time dragging on, filled perhaps with illness, making it longer still, then it's all over. And when things finally get that far, we're left thinking: what a meaningless life."

"Well, meaningless—"

"Meaningless."

He didn't reply. Neither of us said any more. After a while I stood up, regardless of how lonely I felt; I didn't want to share my melancholy with him.

"So long," I said.

"So long, doctor."

Despondency begets sentimentality, and the word 'doctor', uttered without a hint of irony, sent a wave of warmth through me; I turned quickly and hurried away. And right then and there, before even leaving the park, I knew I wanted to die. I wasn't surprised; if anything I was surprised not to be. And at once both the depression and sentimentality seemed to evaporate. I slowed my pace, feeling an inner calm that demanded slowness.

When I arrived home, a feeling of distinct calm still within, I took out some writing paper and an envelope. On the back of the envelope I wrote: *To the judge who sentenced me.* Then I sat down at the small table where I usually eat and began to write down this story.

Today I went to the park for the last time. I was in a strange, almost brash mood; perhaps due to the unaccustomed joy I'd experienced in putting my previous meetings with the judge into words; or, perhaps more likely, because I hadn't wavered in my decision, not for a single moment.

Once again he was sitting there when I arrived. I thought he looked troubled. I greeted him with more friendliness than usual, it came quite naturally to me. He shot me a quick glance, as though to check if I meant it.

"Well," he said, "you're having one of your better days?"

"I have my good days, yes. And you?"

"Pretty good, thanks. So you no longer believe life is meaningless?"

"Oh yes, utterly."

"Hmm. I wouldn't be able to live with such a realization."

"You're forgetting about the sense of self-preservation, a tenacious instinct, which has overcome many a rational decision."

He didn't reply. I hadn't planned on sitting there long, so after a short pause I said:

"We won't be seeing each other again. I came today to say goodbye."

"Really? That's a pity. Are you going away?"

"Yes."

"And you're not coming back?"

"No."

"Hmm. I see. Well I hope you don't think me too forward when I tell you I'll miss our meetings."

"Nice of you to say."

"Time will pass even more slowly."

"There're lonely men sitting on plenty of other benches."

"Ah, you know what I mean. Might I be so bold as to ask where you're going?"

I've heard it said that a man who knows he will die within the next twenty-four hours feels free to do whatever he wants, but that's not true; you are, even then, unable to act contrary to your own nature, your self. Not that giving him an honest, straightforward answer would have been to behave contrary to my nature, but I'd decided beforehand not to disclose my destination to him, as I saw no reason to upset him. After all, he was practically the only person who would be bereaved by my passing. But what should I answer?

"You'll receive word," I said at last.

I noticed he was taken aback, but he didn't say anything. Instead he reached inside his inside pocket and took out a wallet. He looked through it then handed me his card.

"Thank you," I said, putting it in my coat pocket. I felt I should go. I rose to my feet. He stood up as well. He held out his hand. I took it.

"Take care," he said.

"Thanks, likewise. Goodbye."

"Goodbye."

I left. I had the feeling he remained standing, but I didn't turn around to look. I walked calmly homeward, not thinking of anything in particular. Something inside me was smiling. After coming down into the basement, I stood for a while underneath the window looking out at the empty street, before sitting down at the table to finish off this story. I'm going to place the judge's card on top of the envelope.

I'm finished. In a moment I'll fold the sheets of paper together and place them in the envelope. And now, just before it happens, before I undertake the only definitive act a person is capable of performing, one thought overshadows all others: why didn't I do this long ago?

Encounter

THE TREES, the loose sand where the path was most beaten, although people seldom walked there, the ditch with the bridge over it, well, you could hardly call it a bridge: three rotting planks.

"And then?"

"He hit me. I saw only his polished shoes, he always had polished shoes, and a little of his trouser legs. I didn't want to cry out but eventually I had to, he never let up until I shed tears."

A few more meters of path, pine needles, slippery underfoot, then the beach, sand and sea, unchanged, like the time he, like the time I . . . I?

"Did you think you had forgotten?"

"Maybe not forgotten, but time and distance and the fact he sent for me. I'm no longer the same person, you see, at least I thought I wasn't."

"And him?"

"Everything here is just as it was, the setting I mean, and it demands a chain of events that does it justice."

It was low tide, the sand was hard. They followed the windings of the beach. A tree root washed ashore, half buried, an empty bottle, a dead jellyfish pierced by a stick, the smell of seaweed and forest floor, the low sky, it'll soon start to rain, not a breath of wind.

"So you'll be leaving again?"

"Yes."

He didn't hear what she was asking him, he suddenly saw the brown drape, but it wasn't hanging between the two sitting rooms as it should, but was on the balcony outside the bedroom, the blind drawn almost all the way down, the strip of light at the bottom, their legs and voices, the rain on the back of his shirt – "But I'm telling you I've never—" "Oh, you're telling me!" The abrupt movement, his pointy knees, her face just inches from the ground, not a sound, I could have prevented it, could have knocked on the glass, I wanted to, it's not true that I didn't, and in any event how could I know things weren't as they should be, with walls covered in God and shelves filled with Him, making atonement behind the locked door of the broom cupboard, the galoshes and the umbrellas . . .

The pavilion, the dog roses, the meadow, the first drops of rain (you'll get wet, it doesn't matter, your dress, it doesn't matter, here take my jacket, it's so warm aren't you cold?) the raindrops on the back of his shirt. What was I doing on the balcony, in the rain?

"I wasn't the only one," he said. "He beat Mother as well."

"Why?"

"I don't know."

Why? "But I'm telling you I've never—" was that all I heard? Did I run, jump down from the balcony before it was over? I couldn't see what she was feeling, her head was hanging down after all, so it wasn't possible to make out her expression, but she wasn't crying, not while I was looking, I couldn't possibly have seen everything.

"What was she like?"

"Mother? Kind, I think. She would often cry. She never gossiped, at least not as far as I know, and when Father let me out of the broom closet she was never around, I don't know where she got to, but she was never in the sitting room or kitchen. Did you know her?"

"I knew her to see, yes. I remember she had a tendency to blush."

"That's true. I'd forgotten that."

It was striking, hard to miss.

"I remember once," he said, "she was sewing. I think I must have been ill, because sometimes when I wasn't well I was allowed to lie on the couch in the dining room. We didn't say anything, neither of us had said anything for quite a while. Then suddenly she blushed. I lay looking at her, couldn't take my eyes off her, and it was either then or another time I asked her why Father never blushed, but she didn't answer."

The houses, the street running alongside the park with the old linden trees, the rain falling silently, cool against the back of his shirt, the house with the large veranda, the pear trees along the wall (are you coming inside, I should really, perhaps you'd rather come for coffee, I'd like that, thanks for the loan you're probably freezing your back is soaked shall we say around five thanks for the walk) the click of the door latch behind her, the way home . . . home?

He let himself in. He heard his father rattling some saucepans.

"Is that you, Gabriel?"

"Yes."

There was a smell of fish. He went upstairs and changed his shirt. The window was open to the quiet street and low houses. He glanced at GOD IS LOVE in a black frame above the bed. He took it down. Now you're being childish, no I'm not. He put it into the low closet at the end of the bed.

"You coming, Gabriel?"

He took his time. His father had sat down. He was waiting. He put his hands together and bowed his head. Gabriel looked out the window.

"You'll have to make do with what I made."

They sat facing one another.

"It tastes good."

"You have to learn all sorts when you're left on your own."

It didn't taste good, the fish wasn't salted enough. There was no salt cellar on the table, and he didn't dare, I don't dare, that's the way he is, that's the way I am, I've no business being here.

"It's good to have you here again, my boy. It's been empty since your mother passed away."

He didn't reply. The kitchen clock ticked and the tap dripped. It's my turn to say something, what will I say?

"Was she in pain?"

"No. But she would very much have liked to say goodbye to you. She wanted to ask for forgiveness."

"For what?"

"Everybody has something to ask forgiveness for."

"Really?"

"God. . ."

"I wish you'd keep God out of it."

"I won't. I can't."

"Then let's not talk about it."

Silence.

"Have you been to see her grave?"

"Not yet."

"Maybe you could take some fresh flowers from the garden. Are you going there this afternoon?"

"I'm meeting Bodil."

"Who's that?"

"Bodil Karm."

"I see."

"Thank you for dinner."

His father bent his head, put his hands together, and moved his lips, but soundlessly.

"My pleasure."

The flight of stairs up, his room, I stood up to him, the darker patch where GOD IS LOVE had hung, maybe he'll come up and see it, it wasn't raining any longer, a strip of sunlight fell on the mirror, then we can sit on the veranda, footsteps on the staircase, I don't have time to hang it back up, I won't open.

He didn't come in, he went into his bedroom. Gabriel sat down on the bed and felt his heart pounding. I've become the same again, he thought. I can writhe, can take a picture down off a wall, but I'm back in the net. I'm a little sinner again, like I was that time.

That time. The window was open, the curtain stirring gently against the pale evening sky, they couldn't stop caressing each other, the duvet had fallen to the floor, the naked skin, the ticking of the grasshoppers through the window, the faint rustling of the leaves, the steady breathing – *are you cold, no, are you, no* – the soft darkness, the calm movement of her hands now there was no hurry but when there was so much to hold onto, all the softly spoken words, their sense subordinate to their sweet sound – listen to the trees, listen to the grasshoppers, how still it is – long thoughts taking unfamiliar paths, big happy words not seeking answers only echo, her blond hair on the pillow, the fragrances, the July night and her – I could cry, I'm so happy.

And then: the click of the door, the footsteps, the voices, the sudden guilt, panicked moments, her: lock the door, the footsteps on the stairs, the door handle, his father: why have you locked the door, Gabriel? I have a visitor. I'd rather we all settled down for the night now. The shame over his father not even knocking, the fear and the guilt, already intense but only more so on his return after walking her home, it had grown late, his father in the dark in the sitting room: I want to talk to you, Gabriel. Silence. I saw it was a girl, who was she? No reply. It was dark in your room and the door was locked, who was she? I'm not telling you. But I know who it was, I was only asking to give you the chance not to hide something from me, but since you won't spit it out I'm forced to assume the worst and am duty bound to tell her father. If you do. I will. That's rotten. Watch your mouth, Gabriel. It's rotten, rotten.

There was sun on the mirror. He went down the stairs and out of the house, the road was wet and harsh after the rain. He rang the doorbell.

"Mother has gone out for a walk. Make yourself at home. Will you have tea or coffee?"

"Either is fine. Can I sit on the veranda?"

"Sure."

He went out and sat in a wicker chair. She went back and forth. She was humming. He felt a peaceful feeling descend, a mental and physical wellbeing he had of course experienced before, but only rarely.

"You must be happy here."

"You think?"

"With this veranda and this garden."

"It needs looking after, and anyway summers are short. You must have forgotten what it's like here in the winter."

Tea with lemon, crackers with cheese, the distant sound of a chainsaw.

"If you only knew how often I used to walk past here, on the other side of the fence, dreaming about how nice it must be to have a garden like this."

"You had a nice garden yourselves."

"There wasn't a single spot in it that couldn't be seen from the house. I'd nowhere to hide away, neither in the garden nor the house, apart from the basement."

"Didn't you have your own room?"

"Yeah, but I didn't dare lock the door. I wasn't supposed to have any secrets from them and they walked in whenever they pleased, without knocking. I had a desk with drawers you could lock, but I didn't dare hide the key. Granted, I can't actually recall them ever forbidding me from doing it, but then again there was probably no need. What secrets I did have I hid in other places. I remember once I forgot to put my diary away, a little yellow notebook that was easy to hide. I left it out on the bedside table. I must have been fifteen or sixteen, and on the cover I'd written that it was mine and not to be opened by anyone but me. My mother hadn't just opened it, she'd written in pencil at the top of one of the pages: *God sees everything*."

"What was it that actually made you leave home?"

"I don't know. I can't remember. I know that must sound odd, I mean it wasn't that long ago, but I really can't recall. Sometimes I think it was when I saw my father beat my mother, but that can't be right, because I left much later."

"How strange."

"Yes. There's so much I can't remember. There are things I don't know if I've really experienced or just dreamt, and these are things that didn't happen that long ago at all. Other things I remember clearly, but I'm not always able to say when they happened, whether I was eight, ten, or fifteen at the time. But what's strangest of all is that at certain periods of my life I must have had the same dream night after night, until I began to doubt it really was a dream, and that I'd actually experienced it. For instance, for a while I thought I hadn't completed my final exams at school, that I hadn't taken the written exam in English, and not because I couldn't, it wasn't a bad dream, on the contrary, it was a good one, I turned up for the exam but just sat there looking at the others, knowing it wasn't necessary for me to take it, that it was an entirely superfluous exercise and I'd be better off taking a walk in the woods, so I stood up and left. I know this must sound strange, but for a while, I think it must have been for several months, I sort of believed that I really had walked out of the exam hall, even though I knew better of course, I wish I could explain . . ."

"I understand," she said. She got to her feet. "I'll be right back." The feeling of wellbeing had left him. I must ask Father, he's the only one who could tell me, if he can, if he's willing to.

"I have to go," he said.

"Already?"

"I need to talk to my father. Can I call you?"

"I'd like that."

He walked quickly, as though to keep his decision warm. I need to do it now, now or never, I've no reason to be scared, as a child I had a reason because he beat me, now I'm only frightened out of habit, he can't do anything to me, I'm the one who could maybe do something to him, he can just tell me, I'm not afraid of the truth.

"Is that you, Gabriel?"

"Yes."

"Are you back already? Do you want a coffee?"

"No, thanks."

He sat down at the round table in the smaller room. The sun had traveled far westward and sent shafts of light through the north window, all the way to the brown drape.

"I wanted to ask you something."

"Ask away."

"I don't want to dredge up the past, but why – I'm asking because I don't know, I realize that might sound peculiar – but why did I leave home? I mean, what happened that made me leave?"

"Let's not rake up all that. Let bygones be bygones."

"No. I need to know."

"I've tried to understand how it could happen, in what way I failed. Because you mustn't believe that I've put all the blame on you."

"Let's not talk about blame. What do you mean?"

"Perhaps I was too fond of you."

"Is that how you see it?"

"Perhaps I held onto you too tightly."

"You wanted me to be like you."

"Are you accusing me?"

"I didn't want to be like you. Maybe I did when I was small, I don't remember, but not later on. I called you Abraham."

"Abraham?"

"And I was Isaac. As far back as I remember I've been afraid of you, not only because you punished me . . ."

"I never punished you without good reason."

"I used to believe that too once, because I always felt guilty, because I wasn't old enough to tell the difference between guilt and feeling guilty."

"There's no difference between the two."

"There is. Why was Mother always blushing?"

"Let your mother rest in peace."

"She is resting in peace. Why did you punish her?"

"Punish her?"

"You beat her."

"When?"

"I don't know. I saw it. Was it because she was too kind to me?"

"Gabriel! Is this the reason you came?"

"No! No. I shouldn't have come."

"You should have come with a different mindset."

"Just tell me why I left."

"Your conscience should be able to tell you that."

"What do you mean?"

"You didn't leave empty-handed."

"I know."

"Your mother never really got over it."

Gabriel got to his feet.

"I can see I'm not going to get anywhere. You're continuing on from where you left off, playing on my feelings of guilt and hiding behind God. You never punished me without good reason, you say. What reason, what reasons? The same reasons that made the inquisitors wipe out everyone who opposed the authority of the Church? You believe you loved me too much? Measure your love by the hours I spent locked in the broom closet!"

"Do you really think I did that without a heavy heart?"

"I don't know. But you did it with good conscience."

"Yes. Can you say the same about your own actions?"

"No. But the executioners from the concentration camps could say the same about theirs. Does that exonerate them?"

"That's enough, Gabriel. You've said more than I would have put up with from anyone else. One day you'll understand that you've done me wrong. I'm an old man and I might not live long enough to see it, but someday you'll realize . . ."

"Shut up!"

"I am speaking in my own house!"

"Then wait till I've left!"

The hallway, the stairs up, I'm shaking, the bedroom, at least I had my say, I don't feel sorry for him, he'll be spared the sight of me from now on, the suitcase, he didn't win at any rate, whatever winning means, at the end of the day everyone loses, temporary victories are deferred defeats, anyway I didn't come back here to win but in order to avoid defeat for once, I'm not hanging it back up, it will be my final greeting, GOD IS LOVE, in a closet, that's that, not much of a visit, now if only he doesn't, the stairs down, but I can't just leave without saying goodbye, yes I can, because I'm afraid? I'm not running away, I'm departing, should I knock or go right in? I knock, this isn't my home anymore, he doesn't answer, then I'm leaving, he must have heard me, unless he stepped out into the garden.

He opened the door. His father sat in the high-backed chair looking at him.

"I've come to say goodbye."

"You're leaving?"

"Yes."

"This wasn't how I pictured things turning out."

"Me neither."

"I wish I understood you."

He made no reply.

"I was so happy when you wrote to say you were coming."

"I'm sorry it ended up this way."

"Are you?"

"What do you mean?"

"Are you really sorry?"

"I just said I was. I didn't want to fight with you, I didn't even want to prove I was right. Tell me something, Father, say I wasn't your son, say I was just somebody you were acquainted with, and you knew as much about me as you know now, would you have been looking forward to seeing me, to have me staying under your roof?"

"It wouldn't be the same, of course not."

"No. And if you were just a fellow human and not my father, then I wouldn't have come to visit you. But doesn't that mean that mere convention is all that binds us together? We are father and son, in other words we have to show affection for each other, if we don't we feel guilty. But why? Are there any reasonable grounds for believing that devotion is determined by biology? We don't feel any obligation to feel fondness for a neighbor or a colleague, do we? I don't know if you understand what I mean."

"I do, yes. So that's how you see it. As a convention. May God forgive you for what you're saying, Gabriel. Someday you'll realize just how mistaken you are."

"That's what you've always said, as far back as I can remember you've predicted that someday . . . How different everything could have been if you hadn't believed in God."

"Or if you had believed in him."

"Yes. As it is, we're doomed to torment each other."

"Don't blame God for that."

"Not God, the idea of a God, that tenacious myth of a power justifying actions and viewpoints that the future will call inhuman. You believe that God is the purpose of your faith, but that's not true, God is nothing but the belief in God, and that's why God will die, he's dying day by day."

"You're deranged."

"No, I merely represent a future that will renounce a legacy, that will refuse to shoulder the burden of God."

"You should leave now."

"Yes."

He walked toward the door. He placed his hand on the doorknob.

Then he turned and glanced one last time at his father, who sat motionless in the high-backed chair, his eyes closed and his hands gripping the worn-out armrests.

Everything Like Before

THE FAT WAITER was standing well in under the battered, old corrugated iron roof, smoking. It was a little after three o'clock, and the thermometer over his shoulder showed thirty-nine degrees. He tossed the butt away and went into the dim bar where the little Scot was sitting playing patience.

Carl turned and saw a small fishing boat round the long, narrow breakwater. Just beyond, the sea disappeared in a haze of heat.

He sipped his beer, it had become tepid. The fishing boat vanished and everything was motionless.

But only for a moment. Zakarias's little, green Hilux appeared by the corner of the train station. It pulled over and parked beneath the dappled shade of the tousled palm tree. Zakarias got out and began lifting cases of wine and Coke out of the back. The fat waiter came out of the bar and called out something Carl did not understand. Zakarias replied. The waiter worked his fat thighs past one another and walked over to the truck. They began to carry the cases into the bar.

On his way back to pick up more, Zakarias looked over at Carl and called out:

"Hallo. Your wife not here?"

"No. She is sick." He patted his stomach to illustrate his lie.

"Sorry. Good wife – okay?"

"Okay."

They carried in the rest of the cases. Then it was quiet again.

Carl finished his beer, left some coins on the table and stood up. He walked into the alley by the coopers. The shadow from the southwest-facing row of houses was not enough to cover him: the sun burned mercilessly.

He climbed the dark staircase of the guesthouse, up to the third floor. The door of the room was locked. He knocked, but Nina did not answer. He called her name. Nothing. He had been so sure she was inside that he had not looked to see if the key was hanging in the reception. He went down to get it. It was not there.

Damn her, he thought, and went out into the harsh light. He walked back the same way. The table had not been cleared, the coins were still there. He sat down, facing the dark doorway. He put the coins in his pocket. The fat waiter did not appear, and after a while Carl got up and went into the bar where the large ceiling fan made for a hint of a cooler atmosphere. The cook and the Scot were playing chess. Carl asked for a beer. Then he sat down at another table, further in under the corrugated iron roof where the light was not as strong. He was surprised that Nina could be capable of pretending she was not in the room, it was not like her – and in a flash of awareness he realized: I don't know her.

He drank. He thought: I'm going to stay here, she knows where to find me. I'm going to get drunk, slowly drunk.

He drank himself into a state of resentment before reaching a state of indifference, but without getting particularly drunk. People began arriving, and at four-thirty the waiter put on the record player, the siesta was over. The little Scot came out of the bar and sat down at the table closest to the door.

Carl drank, slowly, but willfully.

It was his turn today.

It had been Nina's yesterday.

It had begun so well. They had been sitting at Barbarossa over some fish and a bottle of white wine. The brief twilight came and went, and the soft darkness fell. They talked about how the light seemed to slip out of the narrow streets and gather above the sea before disappearing over the horizon. They drank wine, touched hands, and things were good. The darkness around them grew, they paid and walked towards the old square, hand in hand.

They found a small table outside a café and ordered beer. Nina wanted a raki afterwards, and then one more. Everything was good; Carl had a real feeling of intimacy. Then Nina suggested they move on. They strolled through narrow, dimly lit streets, heading nowhere in particular.

They suddenly heard bouzouki music. They followed the sound, and it led them to a small taverna. The man playing was in his late fifties.

They sat down at the only unoccupied table and ordered raki. There were photographs and newspaper pictures of the man playing hanging up behind the bar. "He must be well known," Nina said, buoyed. She drained her glass of raki and signaled to the skinny old woman behind the bar for another. Carl passed. And all of a sudden Nina was not with him any longer. She was sitting looking around the premises; she had got that peculiar, direct look in her eye – desirous and, at the same time, innocent. She zeroed on three men at a table by the door, either all three or one of them, he did not know. What he did know was that he had to alter, or if necessary spoil, her mood, or else things would turn out badly. But he could not do anything, not right away. When she wanted yet another raki, he asked with a smile – albeit a rather anxious smile – if she intended on getting drunk. "I'm fine," she replied, beaming at the musician and the three men by the door. Shortly after, the old woman behind the bar came over and filled up their glasses, probably at the request of one of the three. Carl said she didn't actually have to drink it, but she did. He followed suit; he had lost. Whatever happens, happens, he thought, it's what she wants after all, it's like she has this urge within her. Nevertheless, shortly afterwards he said he wanted to go. "Are you cross?" she asked, and he denied it, because that did not cover it, he was sad and perplexed, and perhaps a little riled. Yes, ever so slightly riled. He was an abandoned husband right in front of his own wife – damn right he was upset. He motioned to the landlady, smiled and paid, smiled at Nina as well, and at the musician, nobody would be able to tell anything by the look on his face, everything was normal, everything was good. He stood up and asked if she was coming. "Just as we were starting to enjoy ourselves," she said. "We," he said and smiled.

She went with him.

Neither of them spoke. She walked a few paces behind.

They came down to the harbor, and Nina said: "You're not planning on going home, are you?" He equivocated. "I'm not planning on going home," she said. "Only if you don't drink more raki," he said. "Christ, how very kind of you," she said. "Yes," he said. "A beer then," she said.

She picked a table, at the place with the biggest crowd. Carl tried to think of something to say, something to bring her back, but could not. In order to escape the uncomfortable silence, he went to the toilet, and he took his time. When he returned, she had begun talking to two Greeks at the next table; they were speaking in English, asking about Nina – where she was from, where she lived, how long she was staying. They were friendly, not flirtatious, and polite. Carl liked them, particularly the one sitting closest to Nina, who spoke the best English, was called Nikos, and was here on holiday from Athens. After a while, Nina moved her chair nearer Nikos, and Carl, smiling between gritted teeth, said in Norwegian: "You don't need to take a bite out of him." She looked at him. "You have to speak English," she said.

After that he had nothing more to say. Everything took its course. Nina ordered, inadvertently as it were, more beer. Nikos's friend left. Nikos pulled his chair over to their table, Nina placed her hand, inadvertently as it were, on his bare arm. Carl pretended not to notice, or rather, as if it did not mean anything, and carried on the conversation about the trials after the fall of the junta, trials which in Nikos's opinion had been a farce and a disaster. Nina interrupted and asked if he was a lawyer. Nikos laughed, placed his free hand upon hers – but only for a second – and said he worked for an insurance company. Nina said she wouldn't have thought that to look at him. Carl checked his watch and said it was getting late. Nikos checked his watch as well and agreed. He said he was going the same way. They paid. Nina suggested they walk along the beach. Carl and Nikos walked on either side of her. Carl saw Nina taking Nikos by the hand, it pained him. He moved a little away from them, not much, but enough for the small waves on the beach to prevent him from hearing what they were saying. Nina halted abruptly, turned towards Nikos and kissed him on the mouth. It was not a prolonged kiss, and Nikos was merely passive. But he did not let go of her hand. Carl didn't say anything, just stood there looking at them. It was he who had the faint light in his face, theirs lay in darkness. He stood looking at them silhouetted in the lights from the boardwalk, and he saw Nikos withdraw his hand. Then they walked on, nobody spoke. Carl walked a few meters ahead, was not about to turn around, he had some pride. He went diagonally toward the lights, heard them following behind. They reached the road, Carl continued on in the direction of the guesthouse, Nina and Nikos chatting behind him, Nina laughed. Then he turned after all and saw they were holding hands. They were almost at the guesthouse. It's over now, thought Carl, don't crawl, it's over now anyway. He quickened his pace. Nina called out something or other but he pretended not to hear. He entered the guesthouse, nodded to Manos, who was half-asleep beside a small TV, and got the key behind the counter. He hurried up to the room. The balcony door was open, allowing some streetlight to fall into the room. He didn't switch on the lights, but went straight out onto the balcony, which was almost directly above the entrance. He could not hear anything. He leaned over the railing and looked down. They were not there. He sat down, lit a cigarette. After a while he heard the door being opened, he sat motionless, thought for one desperate moment that she was not alone. She was. She stood beside him. "What's wrong with you?" she said. He did not reply. "You're always doing this," she said. He held his tongue, did not answer, because that was what she was out after. "Fuck's sake," she said, and went into the room. He tossed the half-finished cigarette down on the street and lit up another. She turned on the light. "Have I done something wrong?" she asked. He did not reply. She came back out. "Are you not going to bed?" "Not yet," he replied. "Are you going to punish me now?" she asked. "For what?" he replied, thinking it a good answer. "For not being able to satisfy me with that hair-trigger dick of yours." She went back in, turned out the light. He sat there, his heart would not slow, his blood pounded and pounded. Now it's over, he thought, it's got to be over sometime.

He smoked three more cigarettes and presumed she had fallen

asleep. He went quietly in, got undressed, drew the portieres, groped his way to the bed, and pulled the sheet over him. Nina moved. "Is it something I've done?" she said. He did not reply. "Christ, you're such a sadist," she said. He lay for a while, trying to think up the worst thing he could say, and then he said it: "You once told me about a friend of yours who was in the habit of flaunting her cunt. When I looked at you tonight I realized what you meant. You should . . ."

Suddenly she was on top of him, he was caught completely off guard, he felt her fingers close around his throat and heard her hiss: *I'll kill you*. Her grip on his throat was not firm, but he panicked and lashed out. She loosened her grip, but did not stop fighting. He pushed her away, got out from under the sheet and stood on the floor. She lay there gasping for breath. He drew the portiere aside and went onto the balcony, before coming back in again to get his clothes and cigarettes. It was one-thirty.

At two-fifteen he went in and got into bed. Nina was asleep. At nine-thirty he awoke and got quietly up out of bed. Nina was asleep. She had kicked the sheet off. She had a bruise the size of a fist on the front of her left shoulder. For a moment he was almost overcome by a sudden tenderness, but then he remembered. He closed the door quietly behind him.

The fat waiter met his gaze. Carl pointed at the empty glass. The waiter nodded and went into the bar. Carl missed Nina – and hoped she wouldn't come.

Just then she arrived. She was wearing a blue blouse that covered her shoulder.

"There you are," she said and sat down. She smiled slightly. He did not smile, avoided meeting her eyes. As if I'm the one who should have a guilty conscience, he thought.

"I must have been drunk," she said. "Did I go for you?"

He nodded.

"Why?"

"I told you what I thought of you."

"Oh. Right."

The waiter came with a bottle of beer. Nina ordered one too.

"Right," said Carl.

"And what was it you thought of me?"

"That I suddenly realized what you'd meant when you once told me about a girl who flaunted her cunt."

"Oh. Why was that?"

"You don't remember any more than you want to, do you?"

"I remember getting angry and going for you."

"And Nikos?"

"Nikos?"

He related the most humiliating details, except for what she had said about him being unable to satisfy her. He was quite thorough and expected her to be devastated.

The waiter brought her beer just as he was finished saying his piece. She poured it into the glass, slowly, then took a long mouthful, before she said:

"Jesus, Carl. That's nothing to be getting worked up about, I was drunk. And after all, I didn't do anything wrong."

"Right, right. Okay, sure."

"Carl."

"We don't understand one another. What would you say if I'd done what you did?"

"But you're not like that."

"Oh, Jesus."

"But it's important. You're you and I'm me. You don't know me."

"No."

"Don't mock me."

He looked away from her, stared into space and said:

"Just now, before you came, I was sitting here missing you, but at the same time I was hoping you wouldn't come. I felt sort of anxious about you suddenly turning up. As though I ought to feel guilty or even have some reason to. I've experienced it before. Longing for you but not wanting you to come – it's positively schizophrenic. Last night I decided it has to come to an end. I'm sick and tired of being taken advantage of."

"But I was drunk."

"You wanted to get drunk, just like all the other times. And when you're drunk, you invariably walk all over me. I'm not so stupid that I don't realize it's due to something, something in our relationship, something you ought to deal with, but you don't. You suppress it, get drunk, and walk all over me. I'm not a piece of shit, and I'm tired of being treated like one."

"But you never said anything, why didn't you say something?"

"I can't interfere like that, I'm just not able. I don't have any right to you, after all – I only have the right to turn my back when someone toys with me and humiliates me. If I had said more than I did, then it would've just been even more humiliating. I should've left, but I was too pathetic to leave."

She did not say anything. He suddenly felt empty. He poured beer into the glass, even though it was almost full. He wanted to leave. He hoped she would say something hurtful or aggressive to give him a reason to go. But she did not say anything. They both sat on either side of the small table, Carl pretending to look at what was going on around them, Nina with her head slightly tilted and her eyes resting on the green tabletop. A couple of minutes passed. Carl got up and went into the toilet. He stood there pissing and feeling sad. He went back out into the dim bar but he stopped short when he heard jazz music coming from the record player behind the counter. A saxophone was coming over the speakers, singing of a tenderness he was in need of.

He asked for a raki so that he was not just standing there. He could see Nina, he listened to the music and looked at her. He thought: why do I have a guilty conscience?

He drained the glass, went outside, sat down, and said:

"I have a guilty conscience, it's ludicrous, but also a bit sad. It may well be no fault of yours, it could be due to a lack of self-esteem on my part."

It wasn't entirely clear to him why he had said it and what he wanted her to say in reply, but she did not answer at all, just sat there looking straight ahead. And all at once her complaint from the night before, which had not been referred to, planted itself between them, like a fence and like freedom, and as he stood up he said:

"I'm going back home."

He placed a banknote on the table and left. She said something behind him, but he did not catch it. He did not know where he was going. He walked toward the town, into the cluster of narrow streets and lanes. The sun was low, only peeping out between the rows of houses now and then.

He had left her, but she remained stuck on his mind.

When he did not know where he had got to, he sat down at a table and drank raki, ate snails and berated himself harshly. Slave, damned slave, every time you try to exact some justice for yourself, you collapse with compassion for your tormentor!

He drank, and it grew dark, and he got on well with himself. He went from place to place and got drunk. He grinned when he noticed he no longer said 'you' but 'we' when he talked to himself. We'll stay out all night, will we? he said. We'll get drunk and sleep on the beach, that'll give her something to wonder about. To hell with her, we'll sleep right where she stood kissing that damned insurance man. But first we'll get drunk.

And he did.

His memory of the rest of the night was hazy. He vaguely remembered Nina turning up – he didn't know where – and that he refused to go home with her, he was headed for the beach. When he got there he threw up, and it was degrading, he remembered that.

He woke up before noon, at the guesthouse. Nina ran her hand across his chest and through his hair and told him she understood everything.

He knew she did not.

But maybe she understood a little.

Her fingers stroked and caressed, pushing more and more of the sheet away from his body. He remembered, and wanted to resist, otherwise what had been done would be undone. But his desire pressed on, and she saw it and took matters in hand, and there was no way out.

Just before he came, she issued an inarticulate cry, and a prolonged trembling passed through her body. He did not know what to believe, but he knew what she wanted him to believe.

He felt sad and empty.

She lay twirling his hair round her finger.

"Now everything's like before, isn't it?" she said.

He thought about it.

"Yes," he said, "it is."

I'm not like this, I'm not like this

I was descending the stairs of a five-storey apartment building on the east side of town; I'd been to visit my older sister – it hadn't been very pleasant, she had too many problems, most of them imaginary, although that didn't help matters. I've never been particularly fond of her, and she's never held me in very high regard. My reason for stopping by was that one of her problems was real enough: she'd fallen and broken her left hip.

I left her place with mixed emotions. On one hand I was happy to get away, on the other I was annoyed because she'd made me promise to come back the following day.

Anyway, I was on my way down the stairs and between the third and fourth floors I came across a rather old man sitting in the middle of one of the steps, blocking my way. He had placed a large shopping bag between himself and the banister, and as I'm quite reluctant to go down a flight of stairs without having something to hold on to, I stopped just behind his back. He didn't seem to have heard me coming, so after a few moments I said:

"Can I help you with anything?"

As he neither answered nor turned around, I thought perhaps he might be deaf, or at least hard of hearing, so I repeated the question, louder this time.

"No, thank you. I don't think so."

I was taken aback, not by what he said, but by his voice, which seemed familiar; it was very distinctive, deep and sharp at the same time, and most expressive. And it stood in striking contrast to his shabby, almost raggedy, clothing.

Because his voice made me think I knew him, and that he knew me, I succumbed to a fit of vanity. I didn't want to ask him to move the shopping bag, and in so doing show him how unsteady on my feet I'd become, so I let go of the banister and passed him on the opposite side. It went well, but when I turned to look at him I discovered I'd been mistaken. I'd never seen the man before.

I may have looked slightly surprised, and since he couldn't have known why, and in addition was even more shabby looking from the front than from behind, and was no doubt aware of, if not accustomed to, making an unfavorable impression, perhaps that was why he said, half-defiantly, half-apologetically:

"I live here."

"I see."

"I just felt so tired all of a sudden."

As a former photographer I have a certain experience with faces, and as I stood looking at him it occurred to me that his face didn't match his shabby dress either. However, it did match his voice: it had a similar expressiveness.

"Are you sure I can't help you with anything?" I said, feeling I had to say something as I'd been staring at him a little too long.

"No, no, but thank you."

"Well, so long."

I left, and I didn't think there was any reason to hide from him that I held firmly on to the banisters.

The following day I went back to see my sister. I had promised her, and when it comes to keeping a promise I'm a little old-fashioned. But it was snowing heavily and I was tempted to phone and say I couldn't make it. But I went, and she opened her door, resting on her crutches, and asked me to brush the snow off before entering. I refused. I told her I could turn around and leave. At this she moved aside. I went in, hung up my coat, and placed my hat on the hat rack. She hobbled ahead of me to her chair. I sat down on the sofa. I commented on how warm it was in the apartment. She made no reply. Instead she said that the light bulb in the kitchen was out. I couldn't help her with that, I'm prone to dizziness. When I tried to explain to her just how much it affected me, she said no one is that dizzy, that it was all in my imagination. There were a lot of things I could have said to that, but I didn't say a word, there wouldn't have been any point. But she wouldn't let up, she said the causes of dizziness were psychological and in my case were due to my never having dared take on any responsibility. I became cross and got to my feet. I wanted to leave. I'd kept my promise. Now I wanted to go. Maybe she understood that, probably not, in any case she asked me to fetch the tray with Christmas bread and coffee cups from the kitchen, as well as the Thermos flask. I couldn't say no to that. I carried everything in and placed it on the table between us. The slices of Christmas bread were well buttered. "Oh, I say," I remarked in a conciliatory tone, and then she looked happy, which surprised me. She told me she'd baked it herself and I said without conviction that I could tell by the taste. But to be fair it did taste pretty good. Neither of us said anything for a while. I was looking at the snow against the window-pane, wondering what joy my sister could have in life, when, after a while, I reached the conclusion she probably didn't have any and I felt the urge to say something friendly – I simply grew quite sentimental, perhaps due to the snow against the window and the warmth in the room – but I never got around to it because just as I was about to open my mouth she asked if we could play yahtzee. She asked like a child who is all but sure of being refused, and even though I don't really enjoy dice games – they leave too much to chance – she asked in such a way that I couldn't bring myself to say no, and besides I was dreading going outside and facing the snow. She said that the yahtzee pad and the dice were in the desk, and on the wall above the desk hung pictures of my family – it had been a large family, and they were all hanging there, the dead and the living mixed together, it was quite a depressing sight. I found the pad and the dice and returned to the table. We began to play.

Twice in a row my sister threw the dice on the table with such force that one of them fell on the floor, and the second time one of them rolled under the sofa, and while I was down on my hands and knees to retrieve it, she remarked that the seat of my trousers was shiny from wear. I was aware of that, but her commenting on it annoyed me. I've never been able to accept that being related to someone through no fault of my own should justify a lack of tact and I told her as much. "I'm sorry," she said, in a surprisingly meek voice, doubtless worried I might stop playing the game. I didn't say any more about it because just then I remembered the shabby man on the stairway. On my way home the previous day I'd decided to ask her about him, and I was now on the verge of doing so but I checked myself, as I didn't want her to realize I associated him with the seat of my trousers. So I handed her the die and we continued playing. When I figured enough time had passed I mentioned having run into a friendly old man on the stairway who had seemed familiar in some way, and I wondered if she knew who he was? She didn't know who that could have been, and said he must have been visiting someone. There was only one elderly man in the building and he was by no means friendly, he was frightful, and no doubt a homeless person who'd been provided with an apartment through the welfare office. "Yeah, yeah, that's him," I said. She made a big deal out of trying to fix me with an incredulous look but I pretended not to notice and asked if she knew his name. "Larsen," she huffed, "or Jensen, something quite common." Amused at this, I agreed, saying it was not much of a name, poor man. "Now you're being mean," she said. "Just a bit," I replied. "It's your turn." She threw the dice, managing to keep them just barely from rolling onto the floor again. She assured me she was not a snob, whereas I on the other hand was trying to play good Samaritan to a hobo, and it didn't suit me, after all even changing a light bulb was too much for me, and she could just picture my reaction if the apartments in my building began filling up with welfare recipients. That made me angry, I admit it, especially the part about the light bulb, and I was just about to respond in an emphatic, deeply hurtful manner when she threw her head back and burst into tears. She cried with her eyes and mouth open, weeping with such intensity that I realized it was coming from deep inside. I should maybe have gone over and comforted her, placed a hand on her shoulder or stroked her hair, but her statement about the good Samaritan held me back. So I remained sitting, quite at a loss – I didn't understand her terrible sobs, didn't know if I'd seen her cry before, at least not since childhood, she hadn't cried at either Mom's or Dad's funeral, I had never associated her with tears, so I didn't understand this sobbing that went on and on, perhaps not so very long, but it seemed like it, and I grew more and more perplexed, and finally had to ask why she was crying, not primarily to get an answer, no, not to get an answer, but in the hope of making her stop and in so doing putting an end to my own befuddlement. And eventually, after I repeated the question not once but twice, she managed to gasp, in that high-pitched voice people often have after a fit of crying: "I'm not like this, I'm not like this." Then her head fell forward and everything went quiet. I thought: what an unusual way to fall asleep. But she wasn't asleep, she was dead.

Over the next few days I was at her apartment several times, as next of kin it fell to me to make funeral arrangements and settle the estate. On one of my first visits I once again found myself behind the man in the ragged clothes, this time on the way up the stairs. He walked extremely slowly, and I slowed down so as not to end up right behind him, but he must have heard me because he stopped, perhaps to let me pass. He placed both hands on the banister and looked down at me.

"Ah, it's you," he said, sounding relieved.

"You remember me?" I said.

"Of course. Do you live here?"

I stopped three steps below him and explained the situation, and he gazed at me with such an alert look in his eyes that I thought: he's in disguise.

When I'd finished my brief explanation he offered his condolences, then said:

"And to think I wasn't even aware she was dead. I knew her. She was very obliging."

"Well, obliging," I said, "that might be a slight exaggeration."

"No, no, not at all, she even helped me carry a heavy bag full of groceries up to my apartment once."

"Really?" I said, surprised.

"You appreciate that kind of thing, you know."

"Something that should really go without saying."

"Oh, it's ages since that was the case. Times change. You need to set your watch to the correct time. Then you won't be disappointed, that's what I say."

He gave me a faint smile, then turned and continued up the stairs. I followed. He lived in the apartment below my sister's. There was no nameplate on the door. We said goodbye and only when I'd almost reached the top of the next flight did I hear him shut the door behind him.

About a week later I bumped into him on the street. I was returning home after another visit to my sister's apartment. I saw him from a little way off, coming directly towards me, a closed expression on his face, he didn't notice me before I stopped in front of him and said hello, and for a moment he looked like he'd been caught red-handed, but only for a split second, then he smiled. After exchanging pleasantries, I asked, prompted by our standing right in front of a bakery café, if he'd care to have a cup of coffee. He hesitated slightly before saying yes. It was a large and bright place with many round, white tables. He didn't remove his coat, so I left mine on as well. He kept stirring his coffee, even though he didn't take cream or sugar. I had a good many questions on my mind, but I didn't know what to say. Then he asked what my sister died of, and that was a good topic, we were both practically devotees of stroke as a cause of death. The only downside of such a sudden death, he quipped, was that you would have to constantly be putting your affairs in order to guard against leaving any of your secrets, not to mention proclivities, to posterity. I jokingly replied what a vain thought this was, and then he looked at me with a little smile that might have been ironic, and said:

"Perhaps you're not inclined to credit me with any vanity worth mentioning?"

"Yes, of course," I answered, slightly taken aback.

"So you don't judge a book by the cover?" he asked, still wearing that little smile I had trouble interpreting. I assured him that I didn't, not where he was concerned. He looked at me quizzically and I realized I'd said both too much and not enough, and with that I told him there was something about him that made me think he was in disguise.

"You mean," he said, "that I'm someone other than I purport to be?"

"Not exactly," I said, "rather that you've diverged from your starting point, that you've stepped outside a setting, so to speak."

It was clumsily put, and also more forward than I'd intended – I sat feeling anything but comfortable, and the silence that followed was extremely awkward. In the end I said I was sorry, but he waved my apology aside, looking almost frightened, and said I really had nothing to apologize for, on the contrary he had provoked me, besides which I was right to a certain extent, his life had taken a drastic turn some years ago, not that he regretted it, I mustn't think that, if anyone were to ask him whether his life had changed for the better or the worse, he'd simply have to answer that he didn't know, it had merely changed.

After coming out with all these words, which in reality didn't tell me anything at all, he grew silent. I waited for a continuation but it didn't come, and since I reckoned he was too intelligent to say so much without having some purpose behind it, I drew the conclusion that it had been his way of rounding off the topic. Whether I had reason to or not, I felt put in my place and made no great effort to get a new conversation going. We exchanged a few inconsequential words, then he thanked me for the coffee and the chat, and said he had to get going. Outside we shook hands and went our separate ways.

On my next visit to my sister's apartment I'd arranged to meet my younger brother there. I seldom see him and make no apologies for it. He's a legal adviser in a government department and an awfully smug individual. He arrived a half hour after me and twenty minutes later than agreed, admittedly he did apologize, but in such a nonchalant manner that the apology seemed almost like an insult. I bit my lip, and when he'd hung up his coat I handed him a list of the furniture and personal effects. Naturally enough it was the latter he was most interested in, especially whatever there was to be found of jewelry and silver. I had arranged all this relatively neatly on a table between the windows in the bedroom, and when I told him that, he found reason to point out that it was very careless of me not to have placed it somewhere safer, I should know that an unoccupied apartment was a tempting target for burglars. I didn't answer, because I wanted to put off quarreling with him for as long as possible. He went into the bedroom and I walked to the kitchen to put on some coffee. I could hear him through the wall opening drawers and closet doors, and assumed he looked under the mattress as well, as I'd done myself. After a while he entered the kitchen and asked if she'd left behind anything of a more personal nature, letters and such. I replied that they were in the writing desk. He left again, and when I came in with the coffee he was sitting with the rather large bunch of letters in front of him. He was reading. I had read quite a lot of the letters myself, the ones from my mother, one of which I'd tucked away. It contained three sentences about me. I suggested he take the letters home with him to read. He was happy to do that, and I went into the kitchen to find a plastic bag for him to put them in. While I was there the doorbell rang. I heard my brother go to open it. I couldn't remember where I'd seen the plastic bags and it took a little time before I found them. On my way back to the living room I bumped into my brother in the doorway. He looked confused, to put it mildly, and he said, "It's for you." I didn't understand at first how it could be, not before he whispered, "Do you *know* him?" Then I realized who it was, but at the same time was none the wiser as to the shocked, almost distressed, tone of my brother's question. It was him; he was standing outside the door, also looking confused. He apologized – he'd heard footsteps from the apartment, living directly below as he did, had figured it was me, on my own, hadn't meant to intrude, just wanted to ask if, when I was finished, I'd like to have a cup of coffee with him, but perhaps it wasn't a good time as I wasn't on my own. I told him I'd be happy to and he seemed pleased. I went back in to my brother who was standing in the middle of the room looking at me inquiringly.

"Do you know him?"

"Yes, of course I know him."

"Well, that's a turn-up for the books."

"Please, spare me your prejudices," I replied resignedly, but he continued on undeterred:

"And he lives here in the building?"

"Yes, he lives here in the building."

"Gabriel Grude Jensen."

I was taken aback.

"You know him too?" I asked.

"Good heavens, no. But I followed the trial."

"The trial?"

"Yes, the trial. Didn't you say you knew him?"

"He hasn't spoken much about his past."

"No, that I can well understand. He killed his wife, got God knows how many years. Real nasty business."

He said a good deal more, obviously relishing his role as an informant, but when he stooped to sneering at my so-called acquaintance with the man, as he put it, I said I wasn't in the habit of asking people if they'd killed anyone, nor would I allow their answer to play a crucial part in whether I liked them or not.

Following that we did what we had come to do, and after an hour he left. I rinsed the coffee cups, switched off the lights and locked the door behind me, then went down to the next floor and rang the bell. He took my coat and showed me into the living room. It was exactly the same as my sister's in terms of size and layout, but was barely furnished. There was a low, oblong table in the center and on each of the long sides of the table an armchair; behind one of these stood a floor lamp with a dark shade, the light from it just strong enough to reach the almost bare walls. The entire room looked like a stage. He invited me to sit, then asked if he could offer me a glass of brandy with my coffee; I said yes, thank you. I decided not to reveal what I knew about him. When he'd filled the glasses, he asked what I thought of his home. I perceived it as a rather provocative question, partly because of the tone of voice in which he said it, so I answered that the spartan impression it made corresponded either to his disposition or his finances. He said that was what he'd call a diplomatic answer, before adding – rather inappropriately, I thought – that he didn't usually have anything against loneliness. "You mean solitude?" I asked. Yes, yes, that was what he meant. But lately, since my sister passed away, it had grown so quiet; previously he'd heard her footfall, and voices now and again, or sounds from the kitchen – sound carried very easily between the apartments – but now he didn't hear anything and felt at times as though he didn't exist, leading to severe anxiety. Did I also live alone? I nodded. "Anxiety?" I asked. "Yes, you know, when everything turns to an emptiness bearing down on you, and you have to get up and pace the room, even say something into the nothingness, surround yourself with yourself, as it were, it's the only thing that helps." He sipped at his glass. I didn't know what to say – it's not in my nature to confide in others, and when people confide in me it makes me feel uneasy and embarrassed. "Am I being a bother?" he asked. "No, no," I answered, and obviously sounded convincing, because he continued to talk about his anxiety. I felt increasingly uneasy. Even though it didn't show, I assumed he must have had a fair bit to drink before I arrived, it was the most reasonable explanation for him to deviate so sharply from the impression he'd given me on our previous meetings. And when, to top it all off, he began to talk about love, I made up my mind to end the visit. "There's too little love in the world," he said. "We need to have more love for one another." It was very embarrassing. "Who is one another," I asked, "and what is love?" He answered only the first question. "Everyone," he said. I shrugged – I could have refrained, but I felt the need to make a point, and after all it was a rather mild reaction. "You don't agree?" he said. I told him I did not. He thought this was interesting and wanted to top up my brandy. I politely declined, saying unfortunately I would soon have to leave, as I had a previous engagement. But I didn't get up right away, as I didn't want him to see right through me, besides I felt a little guilty, it wasn't as if he'd done anything to me, he had only talked like a foolish priest. So in order to show kindness, I said I hoped it wouldn't take too long to find a buyer for my sister's apartment, so that the silence wouldn't become too oppressive. "Oh, it won't be the same," he said, and when I looked at him quizzically he added, "Your sister had a certain fondness for me." "Really?" I said, perplexed. "Yes," he said, "so knowing they were her footsteps . . . I'm sure you understand what I mean." I nodded and got to my feet. I stood with my face in the shadow of the dark lampshade and nodded and nodded, as though I understood everything – it was a mime, not out of place in the stagelike room. I didn't have a single rational thought in my head. I heard him say it had been a pleasure to talk to someone who understood, a real pleasure, so seldom did you meet a person on the same wavelength. He held my coat for me as I put it on and we shook hands. I left, determined never to set foot in my sister's apartment again.

Mardon's Night

ALL THE STREETS had trade names, Baker Street, Tinsmith Street, Cobbler Street. He put down his suitcase on the wet pavement and took the folded note from his breast pocket. 28 Furrier Street. He continued walking. One of his legs was shorter than the other. His feet and back were cold. I'll ask the first person I meet, but it was a lady, and he didn't ask the next person either. I'm sure I'll find it. The shops were closed but the streetlights weren't yet lit. He came to a bridge and thought he had walked too far, but he continued on. A train whistled below. And there was me thinking it was a river, if a train hadn't come I would've thought I'd crossed a river, and no one would have known where I'd come from. You came from the other side of the river, you don't say? Well, would you look at him, he came from the other side of the river. Was the ferryman drunk today – had he hoisted his daughter up the mast?

He came to a café, a bar, went in and sat in a corner, ordered a cup of tea, placed his hat on his suitcase, and waited. There weren't many customers; if I put them on top of each another, stomach-to-stomach and back-to-back, they wouldn't reach more than halfway to the ceiling.

When the owner came with the tea he asked him where Furrier Street was and he replied that he should continue on over the bridge past a house that looked like it'd had a drop too much to drink and then take the first street to the left and the second to the right, you can't miss it.

He went back the same way he had come, across the bridge, past the house that had had too much to drink, took a left, then a right, but he could not find any street sign, nor any numbers on the row of similar, three-storey buildings. He went into one of them, into a dark hallway with three doors, and an old woman with white hair and a navy apron told him he lived one flight up, his name was on the door, but he wasn't home. He walked up the worn staircase, slowly, with heavy steps, I'm carrying the years with me. He was not at home, but the door was unlocked, and he entered into a cold room with an unmade bed, a table and two chairs. He sat down, rested his head in his hands and thought about the long journey – the train compartment where the widow's son conjugated 'fuck' on his dusty suitcase, sixty hours with no sleep, or next to none, the miner who harped on about Jesus's perversions and after fifty hours cried, Oh Lord, within thy hands – and pulled the emergency brake.

He heard a noise behind him, coming from the door still slightly ajar, open to the hallway, and the other doors with names on them. Oh, I beg your pardon, she said. I didn't know – You must be Lender, he said you were coming, but not today. I'm Vera Dadalavi, I live right across the hall, you can come in and wait, it's warmer in my place, but for goodness sake bring that suitcase with you.

He followed her across the hallway; she had pictures on the walls, drawings of masks, feet, and hands, as well as poems cut out of newspapers, all fastened to the gray wallpaper with green and yellow thumbtacks. He removed his coat and sat facing the door. That's Mardon's hand, she said, pointing at one of the drawings. The index finger was missing. Are you hungry? He was not hungry, just tired. He sank a little further down in the chair and closed his eyes. When will he be home? Hard to say, tonight, tomorrow, whenever he grows weary and can't find somewhere else to sleep. The nights are beginning to get cold. He'll be back.

He looked at the long blond hair, the slender back, the newspaper clippings – I had posters myself, ten thousand days ago, men with banners who strode from continent to continent with sickles in hand. But what was with all the masks? Are you a painter? I dabble, she replied, but I'm no good. Would you like a glass of wine? It was sweet. You look like Mardon when you smile, tell me a little about him, what he was like as a child. Like most children I suppose, he replied, but that wasn't true, he used to catch small birds and lock them in his room with the cat, and when he was eleven he stole books from the bookcase to cover the cost of running away to Australia, nowhere else would do. I didn't know him, he said, he didn't talk much and I was so busy. How is he

– what does he do? Here he comes. She went to the door and opened it. The old man (I'm not *that* old) stood up and wiped his palms on his jacket. He took two steps forward, one short and one a little longer. They looked at each other, in silence. Mardon, Mardon, what have you done to yourself! – then they shook hands, in silence. My hand is clammy, he thought, what will I say, I can't find my voice, he has no index finger, I'm crying, oh God I'm crying. You arrived earlier than expected, Mardon said, I didn't think . . . they both turned at the same time and looked at her. Her eyes were brimming with tears. I can't help it, she said, it was so, after all these years, both of you are so big. They looked away, stared down at the worn carpet. Well, say something, one of you, anything at all. You managed to find the way all right? Yes, but there're no numbers on any of the buildings. They were stolen; no sooner do new ones go up than they disappear. Probably someone who wants people to lose their way. They rob the numbers so people will lose their way? I don't know, but it wouldn't surprise me. Have the two of you been sitting here drinking wine? Yes, your friend has been very kind to me – it was so cold in your room.

They had sat down. I need to go out, Mardon thought, I need to get out and prepare myself for his being here. Poor man, poor bugger, the wart on the side of his nose has grown bigger, he's probably got cancer, he won't be happy until he's dead, I feel sorry for him, if only he hadn't been my father, Father alone on a park bench in the rain, Father crouched behind an armchair in the gloom of the lounge, you didn't think I saw you, Father on the wooden chest at the end of the attic – the almost imperceptible stains on the floor. I need to go out for a while, it won't take long, half an hour or so, just something I forgot. His father stood by the window and watched him hurrying across the street. If you knew how lonely I am, Mardon, you're all I have left. The streetlights were on. Poor Mardon, Vera Dadalavi said, right by his ear. I'm called Mardon too. Really, you named him after yourself? It wasn't my fault, I wasn't home. Do you think he'll come back? Of course, she said and placed her hand on his arm. My father was also called Mardon, he said. I understand, she said softly – come and sit down. Have a glass of wine. Cheers. Cheers. If you're feeling blue it's only due to you having traveled so far, it's so easy to feel down after a long journey, but it'll pass. Are you sure I can't offer you a bite to eat?

When he returned the glasses and the bottle were empty. Here I am, he said, then noticed his father was gone. Where is he? In the lavatory. You've been drinking, Mardon. Here he comes – be nice to him, Mardon, you could crush him between two fingernails. That's a peculiar toilet, his father said, looking like he'd been laughing. Yes, isn't it? Mardon replied. Come, let's celebrate, he said, pulling a bottle from his coat pocket. We've never had a drink together, said his father. You're forgetting the restaurant behind the town square, Mardon said, what was it called again, after the funeral, I was suffering a bout of chills, a little restaurant with deer heads on the walls. We both had two drinks, remember? No, I don't remember. I had other matters on my mind I suppose. There're so many things I've forgotten. Deer on the wall, you say? Yes, I was there after that too, when I was old enough to go in on my own, but by then the animals had been replaced with imitation brick wallpaper, and there was a girl behind the counter with the brightest eyes I'd ever seen – as though she'd come straight out of the sea. She was exceptionally beautiful, from the counter up that is, the rest was dead, she sat on a high stool with wheels on it, they said she'd been run over by a snowcat. What's wrong? Nothing, his father replied, nothing at all. Do you mind if I draw you? Vera asked. No, go right ahead, but I'll soon need to find a place to . . . is there a hotel nearby? Out of the question, you'll take my room of course, it's the least I can do. Fair to say it's no showstopper, I've never bothered doing much with it, but I have clean sheets. I might as well go in now and make it up for you, so it's ready, I mean. It'll only take a moment. I don't want you to go to any trouble . . . but Mardon had already left the room. He makes himself scarce the first chance he gets, as though I were a leper, I wish I hadn't come. Have you ever noticed how nearly all people resemble a type of car? Vera asked. No. You look like a Ford. Me, I look like a Volkswagen Beetle. I'll go in and give Mardon a hand, he said, getting up abruptly. The door was ajar so he pushed it open. Mardon was lying on the bed staring at the ceiling. I suddenly felt so dizzy, he said, I'll be alright in a second. He got up. He's not dizzy, he's just lying there killing time, he doesn't know how to make the minutes pass. It'll just be for tonight, he said, and Mardon said, no, why? He didn't reply, and Mardon thought

I actually feel . . . why do I feel sorry for him? And if I do feel sorry for him why can't I be nice to him? There's no point in me taking your bed – where are you going to sleep? At Vera's. Ah, I see. Yes, of course. He opened a door in the wall and took out clean bedding. I'm his son so he thinks he's fond of me, thinks he has to be. Poor lame bugger, bringing a son into the world does not go unpunished. I wonder what he'd say if I started calling him Mardon. Could you help me put this duvet cover on, Mardon Senior? Here, let me help you, the father said, staring at Mardon's hand. What did you do to your finger? It got infected – not worth talking about. There, that's it. You can do just fine minus one finger, especially an index finger. Should we go back?

She had tied her long blond hair up with a brown ribbon. So, they're sleeping with each other, he thought. She must be at least ten years older than him. I've slept with far too few women in my life, hardly any, didn't dare, they scared me, I called it strong moral principle, you have to call your weaknesses something, so why not strong moral principle, now I know what morality means. How are the neighbors? Mardon asked. Martens, for example? He's dead, didn't you know? Thank God, Mardon said, and his father said, What kind of thing was that to say? I must admit, Mardon said, that there are a number of people I've wanted ten feet underground for a long time – Martens being one, and now he is, cheers. What a thing to say, what has Martens ever done to you? He told tales and spread lies about me – you must've known that – and once . . . Well, it doesn't matter. Martens and Mrs. Bauske, they were cut from the same cloth, but I don't suppose she's dead, is she? She passed away six months ago – from cancer. You'll have to excuse me, but I can't say I'm sorry. What did you mean, his father said, that I must've known Martens told lies about you? I didn't mean it like that exactly, I'm not saying you knew he was lying, but when he told on me you would punish me, without knowing if what he said was true. If that's the case, his father said, looking down at the carpet beside his chair, and Mardon got to his feet, turned away, thinking, I shouldn't have said that, I'm obsessed with dredging up the past . . . I didn't mean to . . . if it had been my intention to hurt him then all well and good. He despises me, the father thought, otherwise he wouldn't have said that. He's been carrying the weight of it all these years and now he's sending me back home with it. I have to say something, Mardon thought, but what? That I don't bear a grudge? People don't say things like that, I don't anyway. You mustn't think I bear a grudge, if I did I wouldn't have told you about it. I know, the father said, that I haven't been a good father to you. Can't we, Mardon said, stop being father and son? Can't we just be human beings, then we can avoid thinking we should have been infallible. If your name wasn't Mardon I would've asked if I could call you by your first name. Why not Mardon? the father said. That, Mardon said, would be like talking to myself. Vera laughed. It's no laughing matter, Vera. Imagine if all people were just human beings, not relatives I mean, with all the special privileges and responsibilities we think we have toward one another. Jesus must have had something similar in mind when he addressed his mother as woman. Cheers, man. The father raised his glass. At the least I need to prevent him from drinking the whole bottle on his own. Cheers, Mardon. How sweet you both are, Vera said. Pay no attention, Mardon said, she only needs to see a kid with a squint and her eyes well up. His father looked down. He's not exactly tactful. So he doesn't like having the same name as me. Mardon Lender the Second and Mardon Lender the Third. Has it ever bothered you, having exactly the same name as your grandfather and me? Mardon gave him a quick glance. Of course, since you ask, I must admit I've often wondered what makes parents name their children after the father. Naturally the two most obvious reasons – and you mustn't take this personally – are that the father, whether he has cause to or not, thinks very highly of himself, or that perhaps the mother is unsure if the child is her husband's son. Don't talk that way about your mother, the father said, straightening up in the chair. Why not? Because . . . He stood up. Let's not talk about it, not now. I'm not . . . I'm not used to drinking. If you don't mind I'd like to go to bed – it's been a long day. He took hold of his suitcase and coat. Of course. I hope you sleep well. I'm sure I will. Goodnight.

Mardon heard the uneven footsteps in the hallway and looked down at the stump of his index finger. The father turned on the light and closed the door behind him. He laid his coat on the bed, set down his suitcase and stood looking around the cold, bare room. Don't you feel sorry for him? Vera asked. Yes, I do, Mardon replied, without taking his

· 95 ·

eyes from the stump. His father went to the window and pulled down a blind full of holes with a picture of a girl sitting on some grass under a tree. Aren't you going to go in to him? Vera asked. He didn't reply. His father looked at the girl in the grass and thought: If he only knew what it was like to have almost your entire life behind you. I don't have the time to wait around for nothing. Mardon filled his glass and drank. I knew it would end up like this, I knew it. What'll I do, Vera? Go to him and say something or other, something that will make him happy, I don't know what, anything, whatever you would've said if you knew he was going to die tonight, the biggest lie you can think of, so that at least you'll know he won't travel home more miserable than he came. Mardon turned and looked at her. His father picked up the suitcase, placed it on the table and opened it. He ran his finger over the topmost of the two albums. I'm only telling him what I actually think, and still it gives me a guilty conscience. Why, Vera? Can you tell me that? Mardon, you yourself have said that conscience is the door to the subconscious, the forgotten. His father took the albums out of the suitcase and opened one of them. Mardon aged five. Mardon in his grandmother's garden. Mardon at the beach. Mardon's first day of school. I should have left out the name. Summer 1948. Jesus, that's Martens standing right behind him, his hand on my shoulder – we weren't *such* good friends. Mardon stood up. I'll go in and ask if there's anything he needs. His father worked the photograph free and put it in his pocket. There was a knock at the door. Come in. I was just wondering if you needed anything. He closed the door behind him. What's that you've got? Oh, just something I took along, I thought you might . . . I made them for myself originally, you can see that by the captions, but if you'd like, it is your childhood after all. He closed the album and took a step back. When you consider, Vera thought, that God doesn't exist . . . Of course, Mardon said, absolutely, thank you so much. Vera unfastened her necklace of dried painted peas and placed it in the glass bowl next to the big green alarm clock. I can't recall ever seeing these photos before, Mardon said. If there are any of them you're not interested in feel free to just take them out. Vera raised her eyes and looked in the mirror. Goodness. Thank you so much, Father. He said father. I said father – he can't ask for more than that. He said father. My boy, my son. She untied the brown ribbon and shook her hair loose, placed her feet slightly apart, picked up the hairbrush, looked herself straight in the eyes, ran the tip of her tongue back and forth along the back of her upper teeth, raised the brush, shifted her gaze from her eyes to a blackhead below the left-hand corner of her mouth, put down the brush, pushed her chin out, pressed an index finger on either side of the dark spot, watched the blackhead snake its way out through the pore, picked it up with her nail, heard footsteps in the hall, wiped the white pulp against her skirt, took her powder puff, then the door opened and Mardon entered with two albums under his arm. The father began to undress under the bare light bulb. He was happy to be given them, that was obvious, he just has difficulty expressing his emotions, gets that from me. So we had a drink together after the funeral, I'd forgotten that, must have meant a lot to him. Mardon tossed the albums on the couch. My past, a loving reminder, without an ulterior motive of course. Take a look. She did. The father put his pajamas on over his underwear, turned off the light and went to bed. He gazed at the cross behind the blind. In three days there'll be a full moon. They're looking at the albums now. I'm not going to be able to sleep. Every time he opened his eyes he stared at the cross. At least you were spared the fleeting years, Maria, the fleeting years and the long nights. You never made it to the stage where you were scared of dying, well, not scared, I don't mean scared. Mardon . . . His heart beat faster, even though he knew it was only his imagination: no one had whispered his name. All I have to do is open my eyes – if I want to I can turn on the light. No need, just think about something else. I have my common sense. They're leafing through the albums. Or maybe they're making love. I would have preferred her a little chubbier, not quite so slim, each to their own, not that I'd say no, but had I been one of those German officers who had the women lined up in front of them and could just point – with a riding whip – then I would have picked one who was petite, a little bit chubby and scared looking. I would've . . . no, that's not true, you picture things you wouldn't do, things you're not capable of doing. If I'm a pig then everyone's a pig. I haven't done anything I regret, I regret only the things I haven't done. I could have had both Mrs. Karm and Charlotte, Mrs. Karm at any rate, there was nothing she wanted more, and Charlotte too. Six or seven prostitutes, and Maria, that's it, and the prostitutes only after drinking to work up the courage. I can't even remember what they looked like. So no one other than Maria. *Mardon* . . . He opened his eyes and looked from the cross behind the blind to the small luminous eye in the door. The room must be bigger than it appears, probably around four meters by three, but now in the darkness it seems considerably . . . We could have played a game of chess, although he probably doesn't play . . . I could turn on the light, just to see what the room actually looks like. I don't remember a stove there, but what else could it be, he couldn't possibly get by without a stove, it'll soon be winter. He should have some pictures on the walls. What an idea to pin up drawings of hands and masks, there must have been a hundred of them, at least. So, I resemble a Ford, do I? He tried to remember what a Ford looked like. Vera laid a quilt over the air mattress. No matter what you say, I can't help feeling sorry for him. Neither can I, though I still wish he were dead. He makes me feel a sort of ridiculous – how shall I put it – obligation. As though I were in his debt. Besides there's something disgusting about him, physically I mean, and I can't think about that night I was conceived – and you can bet it was in the middle of darkest night – it makes my stomach turn. Vera looked at him in astonishment. The father heard a door open and close, and a little while later he noticed that the luminous eye was gone. He listened but could only hear the sound of his own heart. It's beating faster than it should. So weird, Vera said. You mean, Mardon said, you can think about your parents' sex life without feeling, I don't know, discomfort? Sure. The father sat up in bed and listened. It's because of the silence. It was the Japanese, wasn't it, who made soundproof rooms – cells – in very particular dimensions, in order to drive people mad? Not very likely – if they did, the ceilings must have been extremely high. My heart's not beating fast because I'm frightened, it's the other way around – I've traveled too far; the stress has been more than I can bear, and fear is merely a natural result of my heart . . . He lay back down, his face to the wall. He reached out and touched the wallpaper. Yes, the ceiling would have to be very high for it to work, for instance if the floor were two by two meters and it was ten meters up to the ceiling – and not a sound. I could just write a note and leave, explain that I couldn't sleep, tell him I only meant to drop by and say hello, that I'm homesick, without offending him, that I suffer from insomnia, am older than I thought, I'm sure he'd understand, would be only too happy, he doesn't need me, and I don't need anybody who doesn't need me. I could die without anyone shedding a tear. I could write that I'm grateful to him for being so friendly and welcoming and that I hadn't actually planned on staying over, but didn't want to reject his offer, but I can't sleep and the train leaves early in the morning. I only wanted to see you and now I have. I have to get back to where I belong, where my things are, that's how it is to grow old, that's what it's like to know that you'll soon be finished. When I was young I thought death became less and less frightening the older you got, simply because it had to be that way if you were to endure it at all, but that's not true, it's a lie. Maybe not for everyone, not for those who have helped themselves, who have never passed up an opportunity, so if I were to give you a piece of advice, Mardon, it would be to never miss an opportunity, take what you can get, even if you risk being accused of ruthlessness – if you're what people term considerate, you end up as a middle-aged man, then an old man, in an attic. You saw me, oh God, I'd forgotten, how could I forget. Maybe you were too small to understand, but you saw me that afternoon in the attic. He withdrew his hand, sat up in bed again, saw the cross behind the curtain, felt his heart beating and a blush burning his cheeks and forehead, stood up, groped for the light switch, couldn't find it, but this is where it was, or maybe on the other side of the door, no, but take it easy, it's here someplace, but he couldn't find it. He went to the window and pulled at the blind. At first it was reluctant, then it slipped out of his hands and rolled up with a clatter, sending a hot burst of fear through him. He stood for a moment as though frozen, then put his hands on the windowsill and leaned his head against the middle glazing bar. I hardly remember her, Mardon said, even though she lived until I was fifteen. She hasn't left behind any traces – if she has, they're hidden. She has no hold on me, if you know what I mean. He hesitated, before saying: I think people who remember have greater control over their lives. These photographs say practically nothing to me. I could tell you about a hedge with white berries that popped when I squeezed them, or about the dusty sods of grass on the left-hand side of the road to primary school – they're my memories. And about Father, but that must have been later on. I once saw him while he was sitting in the attic masturbating, it must have been before Mother died. I'd like to know how I reacted – back then. Later it made him more human in a sense – gave him an extra dimension, if you understand what I mean. He didn't see me, if he had it would have made things a lot more difficult. And one time – I remember this very clearly – I saw him sitting on a bench in the rain, on his own. I pretended not to have noticed him. Why would a man sit on a bench in the rain, less than three hundred meters from his own home? She didn't answer. The father straightened up and turned to face the room. He went over to the door, located the light switch and turned it. Then he walked back and pulled down the blind, without looking at the girl in the grass. He took off his pajamas and dressed, quickly – as though he had no time to lose. He then placed the pajamas in the suitcase and closed it. Once he was done, he stood staring into space, as if he had plenty of time all the same. Mardon lit a cigarette and said: We can't actually do anything about who we are, can we? We're completely at the mercy of our pasts, aren't we, and we didn't have a hand in creating our pasts. We're arrows flying from the womb and landing in a graveyard. And what does it matter how high we flew at the moment we land? Or how far we flew, or how many we hurt on our way? That, Vera said, can't be the whole truth. Then show me the rest of it. His father opened his wallet and took out the light blue receipt from the travel agency, then sat down and began to write on the blank reverse. Dear Mardon. I'm going home again on the train that leaves in a few hours. I very much wanted to see you again and I'm so happy I came. But I'm older than I thought and the long journey has tired me out. If I could only get to sleep, but I'd forgotten the effect unfamiliar rooms have on me, and my heart is not what it was. I'm sure you'll understand. I hope things turn out well for you, my boy. Your loving father. He placed the letter on the table then went to the door, turned off the light, and opened the door carefully. The hallway lay in darkness. He closed the door again and turned on the light in the room. Perhaps they haven't fallen asleep. He opened the door wide so that the light from the room fell all the way to the staircase. He could hear a distant, indistinct mumbling. Yes, yes, yes, I feel sorry for him, I do. Why not feign a little love, if only for a day, not just for his sake but for your own. He began to creep toward the stairs. Feign love? It sounds so easy. He held onto the banister with his right hand. The ground-floor hallway lay in darkness. When he gave me the albums I called him father. I could see how happy it made him, and when I saw that I hated him. What has he done to me seeing as I can't even bear making him happy? He walked slowly – it grew darker and darker. It was as though he unburdened himself at each step. He drew close to the door, feeling his way step by step, groped for the doorknob and opened. I'm on my way home. Or, what have you done to him? Vera asked – she had turned off the light. She was lying on the air mattress, her hands resting underneath her cheek. What do you mean? Just that it's usually the debtor who harbors hatred for the creditor, not the other way around. He smiled as he walked along in the middle of the quiet street, on either side the houses without numbers, to think someone would steal them, I'll be home in two days, I'm on my way. I remember, she said, a person doing me a big favor once. I should've thanked her, I owed her that much, I thought, but I didn't, and instead put it off until it was too late, and then one day I heard she was dead. Do you know what I felt? Relief. Hold on, I didn't come this way, let me see, I came from the east, best to get away from these side streets, you never know what might happen, a black cat, that means luck. I'm not superstitious. God knows where I'm going to end up. This street looks pretty seedy – better off staying in the middle of the road. I definitely haven't been here before. Why do I think I came from the east – and if I did, which way is east, in the middle of the night? Well, I've loads of time, I can always go west – I'm bound to come across something other than black cats sooner or later. Tell me, Mardon said, what I should do. She didn't reply. She was crying. Why are you crying, Vera? He heard footsteps behind him. He speeded up his pace, wanted to turn around but didn't, walked diagonally toward the pavement on the left – what does he think I'm doing here so late at night, with a suitcase, in the middle of the street? Mardon kneeled down beside the air mattress. Tell me why you're crying, Vera. The footsteps are drawing closer, he thought. He looked back, but there was no one there, and when he stopped, the footsteps died away. He turned, walked back the way he had come, and immediately heard the footsteps again. I'm accompanying myself. Mardon stroked her wet cheek. Tell me, Vera. She raised her head and looked at him. I'm just being silly, she said. He could barely discern her features. Let's make it enjoyable for him, Mardon. Yes. He laid his cheek against hers and closed his eyes. The father came out onto the wide shopping street and turned left, toward the train station.

Midsummer

$\ldots$ A<small>ND ALTHOUGH IT</small> wasn't yesterday, I remember clearly that we were lying on our stomachs knocking the heads off plantains and that it was the middle of summer without a cloud in sight but a strong wind from the west, coming off the North Sea, and the only thing to be seen in the sky besides the sun was the occasional seagull. Hans said he was thirsty, but we continued flicking the flowers off the plants, each of us. It was between four and six in the afternoon, and at one point Karl, or Kalle as he was known for short, stood up briefly before quickly lying down again to seek shelter from the wind, the shelter the ground itself gave, because nothing else grew on the plain apart from grass, plantains, pansies, and a small white flower without a name. I didn't know back then what a meadow like that could mean, that you could carry it within you and seek repose, whether in a city apartment or an office on a winter's day; I wasn't lying there feeling happy, I was just lying there, between the town and the sea, in short pants and a plaid shirt with rolled-up sleeves with a pile of plantains thirty centimeters from my face, together with Kalle and Hans, who we sometimes called Lazarus, although I never knew why. Then we heard the siren; we raised our heads but didn't see anything, looked all around to no avail, hoping against hope, sat up, turned our backs to the wind and stared in the direction of town and shouted in unison when we saw the smoke. Then we began to run. Hans in front with his long, skinny legs, and Kalle at the rear, and when he called out for us to wait we pretended not to hear, he was too fat and flat-footed, and soon there was a gap of twenty meters between Hans and me and another fifty back to Kalle, and the smoke grew thicker and thicker all the time, but the siren no longer wailed.

I ran across the football pitch and through the schoolyard, past Hans who had stopped to take a drink from the green fountain, past the white window frames of the classrooms, before Hans caught up with me, his chin was wet, and I couldn't make out what he said as he passed, my shoelace had come undone and while I bent down to tie it in the street outside Rosenstand the bank manager's white picket fence, I heard Kalle approaching. Having already come to a stop, I waited, so I was beside him when we rounded the corner at Bach's pastry shop and saw the flames break through the roof of the narrow two-storey house that was his home and from where you could see the sea, the horizon, and glimpse the light from the larger of the two lighthouses from the attic window.

Was Karl smiling or fighting back tears? And why did he begin walking at an angle, leading with his right shoulder, sort of sideways, and why did he stop at the stoop outside Schmidt's and stand there right up until the roof collapsed and all hope was lost? I'm not asking myself that now, I was asking back then, even though it would have been just as natural to ask why not, after all, it's small wonder you might behave in an odd way when your house is burning down, along with everything in it: your bird eggs, butterflies, and stamp collection.

I won't dwell on the fire, we've all put some fire behind us after all, and this one took place in the afternoon, on a sunny day, lacking in any otherworldly effect it might have had if it'd occurred around midnight, and besides, since the wind was blowing in a westerly direction, there was very little risk it would spread to the neighboring houses.

It must have been two or three days later, because as we walked by the site of the fire all the embers were extinguished and the ashes cold; a hot day, hardly a breath of wind, close to five o'clock; Hans hadn't seen Karl since outpacing him on the plain and I hadn't seen him since he stood helplessly or despairingly or captivated by Schmidt's stoop, but we knew that he and his parents had moved in with an uncle on the east side of the river. The ashes were, as I said, cold, and we continued along by Rosenstand the bank manager's white picket fence and into the school yard where Hans went over to the green fountain and after he'd drank we clambered up onto the corrugated iron roof where we could lie on our stomachs in the shade and look down on the park, which just at that moment lay empty under the tall elm trees. It was a half-dead day, and we were probably bored, I don't think we had much to say to each other, I don't think we were children any longer even though we weren't more than fifteen, it occurs to me I hardly said a word that whole summer and didn't hear what other people said, that all sounds were distant sounds but that it was sunny and warm day in and day out, but be that as it may, what matters if anything does matter is how I think it was, and that's how it was. And when we'd been lying on the corrugated roof for a half hour or maybe more we saw him, I spotted him first, coming from the direction of the park where the drainage ditch was, a ditch without runoff, looped in a horseshoe shape around two huge trees that were crooked and decaying but protected by a preservation order and supported by two thick stakes. There was no water in the ditch that summer, and if you jumped down into it you could stand up straight without being seen from the path, and that was the way Karl came. He looked around but that didn't necessarily mean he had anything to hide and if he hadn't fallen over, which he did, we probably would have called out to him or at least not hidden, but when he fell he remained lying on the ground, although he could hardly have hurt himself, and so we didn't say a word, just watched. He just lay quite still to start with, then we heard him crying, and we made ourselves as small as we could up on the corrugated iron roof. He wasn't crying uncontrollably, and if his home hadn't just burned down we might've thought he was lying there humming, but he wasn't, because after a little while he got to his feet and we saw him wipe his eyes. He walked straight toward us, but it was too late to make our presence known, we stayed out of sight, and couldn't see him anymore but could hear him, followed the sound of him step by step until he came to the covered school entrance. Then the footsteps stopped and were replaced by a new sound: the soles of his shoes as he climbed up onto the broad beam and into the coach house right below us. We had only a thin layer of corrugated iron and at the most two or three meters of air separating him from us, and at first we heard him breathing, then begin to cry, before he turned quiet for a few minutes, and it occurred to me that the only way we could get away without being seen was to run along the roof and jump down into the caretaker's garden. I signaled to Hans what I was thinking, and he shook his head at first because he was probably more frightened of the caretaker than of Karl, but he soon changed his mind and we ran as fast as we could along the long roof and jumped down onto the lawn in front of the kitchen window and ran out the gate, and didn't close it again behind us, just ran and ran, Hans in front and me behind, until we reached the quay. There we tried to laugh at what Karl must have thought, because it must have made a tremendous racket when we ran across the corrugated iron roof, but we couldn't quite manage (something that also suggests that we weren't children any longer) because we felt guilty, or at least I did, although even today, not so long after, I ask myself what else we could have done.

The following day shimmered with heat again. I walked alone through the park, across the square and into the woods. I don't think I was headed anywhere in particular, although the path did lead to Fladen Strand, where I usually took a dip on my own because I couldn't swim properly, and the reason I might not have made it that far was because a little off to the left of the path I spotted the beer bottles, one at first, then one more, then another, far too many for me to manage to carry home. I hid them in some undergrowth in the crevice of a rock and set off for home to fetch something to carry them in, taking the quickest route, which meant leaving the woods and going across the plain, and there he lay, on his side, with his knees pulled up, as though he were asleep, but he wasn't, and he turned toward me, a strand of grass between his lips. His gaze made me feel so guilty that I immediately shared news of my discovery of the empty bottles with him, they were the straw I clutched to, with a stream of words, making the most of them I could, turning ten bottles into fifteen, but he was barely listening, and said he had to go home. We walked side by side, talking of course, but not about the fire, not until he said: We're going to build a new house with a garden and a hedge around it. I reacted as though he'd presented me with a miracle, I wanted to hear the details – at which point he turned strange and said: You won't tell anyone, will you? No, of course I won't. He fell silent, making me go quiet, I couldn't even bring myself to ask why it should be a secret, he had an advantage over me by virtue of the fire, or perhaps due to his crying, I was guilty of having run across a corrugated iron roof, he was the one deciding, and neither of us said any more before making it to the newly planted forest, where the highest pine trees reached to our chests, then he asked if I knew what Judgement Day was. I told him what I knew, how one day the world would suddenly end in some way or another, one day when no one was expecting it, a storm nobody had ever seen the likes of would come or an earthquake would allow all the fire within the earth to rise up through the cracks, and nobody would escape, not one single person. When no one's expecting it? he asked, and I didn't realize that he was asking for reassurance, for a yes, I was very forthright and answered that perhaps one or two people would be expecting it, there was always someone who was expecting it, but most people weren't. I don't think we spoke after that, or at least he didn't ask any more questions. We had walked through the newly planted forest and up onto the road between the filling station and the deacon's garden, and were about to go our separate ways; he dithered a little, or rather, he kicked a sod growing out from under the wire fence loose, then he left.

Days passed where nothing seemed to happen, one hot, cloudless day merging with the next. I spent hour after hour in my spot at the edge of the garden, beneath the biggest plum tree, on my stomach on the grass, happily unhappy, fifteen years old.

Then one afternoon Kalle came walking down through the garden. He sat down on the grass, his large face glistening with sweat. He was silent for a while, then without preamble he asked if I believed in God.

Of course.

I don't, he said.

I looked at him. I'd seen many people who lived as though they didn't believe in God, but had never heard anyone say it. I knew there was a sin, had heard tell of a sin, for which there was no forgiveness, a mortal sin, I'd never had the courage to ask Mother or Father what it was exactly, asking them that kind of thing was as unthinkable as asking them to tell me how I came into being, but I had an idea that was precisely this: denying God's existence – this was a sin which was unpardonable, which fastened the millstone around the neck of the damned.

I lay there growing frightened. Hell drew very close.

You don't know what you're saying, I said.

I do.

Imagine you go to hell.

There's no such thing. We just die.

Why do you think we're born then, if we're only going to live a certain amount of time, and after that there's nothing else?

I don't know. Do you believe that maybe ants and flies go to heaven as well?

They're not created in God's image.

He didn't reply. I thought I'd caught him out.

I read someplace, he said, that people don't love God, they're only afraid of hell.

That's not true.

So you're not afraid of hell?

I am, but . . . but if something frightens you, then you'll try to find your mother or father, and that doesn't mean you don't love them.

That's different. You'd do that even if you didn't love them, as long as you knew they loved you.

He turned to me, his face was no longer glistening with sweat, it was red and blotchy. He looked scared.

Will you come up to the Calotte with me? he asked. I want to show you something.

We walked through the garden and out onto the road. He wouldn't say what he was going to show me, and I didn't nag him to find out. We walked in silence through quiet late afternoon streets, on the right-hand side, in the shade of hedges and trees. It must have been close to six o'clock, at any rate Klipper's forge was closed, and he didn't usually go home before around that time. I remember because we took the shortcut across his property and clambered up the steep slope to the narrow ledge along the rock face where we had to walk in single file. We emerged onto a two- or three-meter-wide plateau where we could see the ocean and the lighthouse. About eight or ten meters below the plateau, lay the concrete yard behind the chapel.

Karl stopped and brushed the fringe away from his forehead. He was sweating again. He stood for a while staring in the direction of the site of the fire. I began to grow impatient. I'd followed him up there because I wanted to do a good deed and now I thought it was time he asked for help.

Do you think God could have prevented the fire? he asked.

Yes.

He was standing in the center of the plateau, over a meter from the edge.

Is it true that God cannot be mocked?

Yeah.

He looked at me. He was scared. He was standing with his back to the sea and the rooftops. He took a small step backward. I stood as though nailed to the spot, I felt dizzy, it always happens, I can't bear to look at people balancing on the brink of a precipice, but unbearable as it is I'm fascinated by it, and I didn't turn away. He took another step backward and stood just a few centimeters from the edge, still with his back to it. I knew heights made him just as lightheaded as me. We stared at each other, I think I meant a lot to him at that moment. He was so afraid – and so brave!

I mock God, he said, or whispered rather, the words hardly reached me. His lips continued to move but I couldn't hear any more. Then he turned and looked down, giving God the best card he held, his dizziness. I don't know how long he stood there, long enough, longer than I would have managed to stand there to prove the opposite, that God existed and I dared to put my life in his hands.

Then it was over. He didn't exult in his triumph. He didn't look at me. Without a word we went back the same way we had come, along the narrow ledge and down behind Klipper's forge. He walked with his head bowed – as though he were ashamed. He didn't say a word, not even goodbye when we got to where our paths diverged, just went on his way while I remained standing there. I watched him go, he was wearing short pants that came down to the back of his knees. I saw him disappear around the corner, then I turned and set off in the direction of home, walking slowly, on the left-hand side of the street, in the shade of the trees and hedges.

The Dogs of Thessaloniki

W E DRANK morning coffee in the garden. We scarcely spoke. Beate got up and put the cups on the tray. We should probably take the chairs up onto the veranda, she said. Why? I asked. It looks like rain, she said. Rain? I said. There's not a cloud in the sky. There's a nip in the air, she said, don't you think? No, I said. Maybe I'm mistaken, she said. She walked up the steps onto the veranda and into the living room. I sat there for another quarter of an hour, and then carried one of the chairs up to the veranda. I stood awhile looking at the woods on the other side of the fence, but there was nothing to see. I could hear the sound of Beate humming through the open door. Of course, I thought, she must have heard the weather forecast. I went back down into the garden and walked around to the front of the house, over to the mailbox beside the black wrought-iron gate. It was empty. I closed the gate, which for some reason or another had been open; then I noticed someone had thrown up just outside it. This got me a little riled. I attached the garden hose to the tap by the cellar door, turned the water on full, and dragged the hose after me over to the gate. The jet of water hit at slightly the wrong angle and some of the vomit spattered into the garden, the rest spread out over the asphalt. There were no drains nearby, so all I succeeded in doing was moving the yellowish substance four or five meters from the gate. Even so, it was a relief to get a bit of distance from the filthy mess.

When I'd turned off the water and coiled up the hose, I didn't know what to do. I went up the veranda and sat down. After a few minutes I heard Beate begin to hum again; it sounded as though she was thinking about something she liked thinking about, and probably thought I couldn't hear her. I coughed, and it went quiet. She came out and said: I didn't know you were sitting here. She had put on makeup. Are you going somewhere? I asked. No, she said. I turned my face toward the garden and said: Some idiot's thrown up outside the gate. Oh? she said. A proper mess, I said. She didn't reply. I stood up. Do you have a cigarette? she said. I gave her one, and a light. Thanks, she said. I walked down from the veranda and sat at the garden table. Beate stood on the veranda smoking. She threw the half-finished cigarette down onto the gravel at the bottom of the steps. What did you do that for? I said. It'll burn up, she said. She went into the living room. I stared at the thin band of smoke rising almost straight up from the cigarette; I didn't want it to burn up. After a while I stood up, I felt unsettled. I walked down to the gate in the wooden fence, crossed the narrow patch of meadow and went into the woods. I stopped just inside the edge of the woods and sat down on a stump, almost concealed behind some scrub. Beate came out onto the veranda. She looked toward where I was sitting and called my name. She can't see me, I thought. She went down into the garden and around the house. Then walked back up onto the veranda. Once again she looked in the direction of where I was sitting. She can't possibly see me, I thought. She turned and went into the living room.

When we were sitting at the dinner table, Beate said: There he is again. Who? I said. The man, she said, at the edge of the woods, just by the big . . . no, now he's gone again. I got up and went over to the window. Where? I said. By the big pine tree, she said. Are you sure it's the same man? I said. I think so, she said. There's nobody there now, I said. No, he's gone, she said. I went back to the table. I said: Surely you couldn't make out if it was the same man from that distance. Beate didn't reply right away, then she said: I would have recognized you. That's different, I said. You know me. We ate in silence for a while. Then she said: By the way, why didn't you answer me when I called you? Called me? I said. I saw you, she said. Then why did you walk all the way around the house? I asked. So you wouldn't realize I'd seen you, she said. I didn't think you saw me, I said. Why didn't you answer? she said. It wasn't really necessary to answer when I didn't think you'd seen me, I said. After all, I could have been somewhere else entirely. If you hadn't seen me, and if you hadn't pretended as if you hadn't seen me, then this wouldn't have been a problem. Dear, she said, it really isn't a problem.

We didn't say anything else for a while. Beate kept turning her head and looking out the window. I said: It didn't rain. No, she said, it's holding off. I put down my knife and fork, leaned back in the chair and said: You know, sometimes you annoy me. Oh, she said. I'm often wrong. Everybody is. Absolutely everybody. I just looked at her, and I could see that she knew she'd gone too far. She stood up, took hold of the gravy boat and the empty vegetable plate and went into the kitchen. She didn't come back in. I got to my feet as well. I put on my jacket, then stood for a while, listening, but it was completely quiet. I went out into the garden, around to the front of the house and out onto the road. I walked east, away from town. I was annoyed. The villa gardens on both sides of the road lay empty, and I didn't hear any sounds other than the steady drone from the motorway. I left the houses behind me and walked out onto the large plain that stretches all the way to the fjord.

I got to the fjord close to a little outdoor café and I sat down at a table right by the water. I bought a glass of beer and lit a cigarette. I was hot, but didn't remove my jacket as I presumed I had sweat patches under the arms of my shirt. I was sitting with all the customers in the café behind me; I had the fjord and the distant wooded hillsides in front of me. The murmur of hushed conversation and the gentle gurgle of the water between the rocks by the shore put me in a drowsy, absentminded state. My thoughts pursued seemingly illogical courses, which were not unpleasant, on the contrary I had an extraordinary feeling of wellbeing, which made it all the more incomprehensible that, without any noticeable transition, I became gripped by a feeling of anguish and desertion. There was something all-encompassing about both the anguish and feeling of desertion that, in a way, suspended time, although it probably didn't take more than a few seconds before my senses steered me back to the present.

I walked home the same way I had come, across the large plain. The sun was nearing the mountains in the west; a haze lingered over the town, and there wasn't the slightest nip in the air. I noticed I was reluctant to go home, and suddenly I thought, and it was a distinct thought: if only she were dead.

But I continued on home. I walked through the gate and around the side of the house. Beate was sitting at the garden table; her older brother was sitting across from her. I went over to them, I felt completely relaxed. We exchanged a few insignificant words. Beate didn't ask where I had been, and neither of them encouraged me to join them, something that, with a plausible excuse, I would have declined anyway.

I went up to the bedroom, hung up my jacket, and took off my shirt. Beate's side of the double bed wasn't made. There was an ashtray on the nightstand with two butts in it, and beside the ashtray lay an open book, facedown. I closed the book, brought the ashtray into the bathroom and flushed the butts down the toilet. Then I undressed and turned on the shower, but the water was only lukewarm, almost cold, and my shower turned out to be quite different and a good deal shorter than I'd imagined.

While I stood by the open bedroom window getting dressed, I heard Beate laugh. I quickly finished and went down to the laundry room in the basement; I could observe her through the window there without being seen. She was sitting back in the chair, with her dress hiked far up on her parted thighs, and her hands clasped behind her neck making the thin material of the dress tight across her breasts. There was something indecent about the posture that excited me, and my excitement was only heightened by the fact she was sitting like that in full view of a man, albeit her brother.

I stood looking at her for a while; she wasn't sitting more than seven or eight meters from me, but because of the perennials in the flower-bed right outside the basement window, I was sure she wouldn't notice me. I tried to make out what they were saying, but they spoke in low tones, conspicuously low tones, I thought. Then she stood up, as did her brother, and I hurried up the basement stairs and into the kitchen. I turned on the cold-water tap and fetched a glass, but she didn't come in, so I turned off the tap and put the glass back.

When I'd calmed down, I went into the living room and sat down to leaf through an engineering periodical. The sun had gone down but it wasn't necessary to switch the lights on as yet. I leafed back and forth through the pages. The veranda door was open. I lit a cigarette. I heard the distant sound of an airplane, otherwise it was completely quiet. I grew restless again and I got to my feet and went out into the garden. There was nobody there. The gate in the wooden fence was ajar. I walked over and closed it. I thought: she's probably looking at me from behind the scrub. I went back to the garden table, moved one of the chairs slightly so that the back of it faced the woods, and sat down.

I convinced myself that I wouldn't have noticed it if there had been someone standing in the laundry room looking at me. I smoked two cigarettes. It was beginning to grow dark, but the air was still and mild, almost warm. A pale crescent moon lay over the hill to the east and the time was a little after ten o'clock. I smoked another cigarette. Then I heard a faint creak from the gate, but I didn't turn around. She sat down and placed a little bouquet of wildflowers on the garden table. What a lovely evening, she said. Yes, I said. Do you have a cigarette? she said. I gave her one, and a light. Then, in that eager, childlike voice I've always found hard to resist, she said: I'll fetch a bottle of wine, shall I? – and before I'd decided what answer to give, she stood up, took hold of the bouquet and hurried across the lawn and up the steps of the veranda. I thought: now she's going to act as if nothing has happened. Then I thought: then again, nothing has happened. Nothing she knows about. And when she came back with the wine, two glasses and even a blue-check tablecloth, I was almost completely calm. She had switched the light on above the veranda door, and I turned my chair so I was sitting facing the woods. Beate filled the glasses, and we drank. Mmm, she said, lovely. The woods lay like a black silhouette against the pale blue sky. It's so quiet, she said. Yes, I said. I held out the cigarette pack to her but she didn't want one. I took one myself. Look at the new moon, she said. Yes, I said. It's so thin, she said. I didn't reply. Do you remember the dogs in Thessaloniki that got stuck together after they'd mated, she said. In Kavala, I said. All the old men outside the café shouting and carrying on, she said, and the dogs howling and struggling to get free from one another. And when we got out of the town, there was a thin new moon like that on its side, and we wanted each other, do you remember? Yes, I said. Beate refilled our glasses. Then we sat in silence for a while, for quite a while. Her words had made me uneasy, and the subsequent silence only heightened my unease. I searched for something to say, something mundane and diversionary. Beate got to her feet. She came around the garden table and stopped behind me. I grew afraid, I thought: now she's going to do something to me. And when I felt her hands on my neck I gave a start and lurched forward in the chair. At almost the same instant I realized what I had done and without turning around, I said: You scared me. She didn't answer. I leaned back in the chair. I could hear her breathing. Then she left.

Finally I got up to go inside. It had grown completely dark. I had drunk up the wine and thought up what I was going to say – it had taken some time. I brought the glasses and the empty bottle but, after having thought about it, left the blue-check tablecloth where it was. The living room was empty. I went into the kitchen and placed the bottle and the glasses beside the sink. It was a little past eleven o'clock. I locked the veranda door and switched off the lights, and then walked upstairs to the bedroom. The bedside light was on. Beate was lying with her face turned away and was asleep, or pretending to be. My duvet was pulled back, and on the sheet lay the cane I'd used after my accident the year we'd got married. I picked it up and was about to put it under the bed but changed my mind. I stood holding it while staring at the curve of her hips under the thin summer duvet and was almost overcome by sudden desire. Then I hurried out and went down to the living room. I had the cane with me and without quite knowing why, I brought it hard down across my thigh, and broke it in two. My leg smarted from the blow, and I calmed down. I went into the study and switched on the light above the drawing board. Then I turned it off and lay down on the sofa, pulled the blanket over me and closed my eyes. I could picture Beate clearly. I opened my eyes, but I could still see her.

I woke a few times during the night, and I got up early. I went into the living room to remove the cane, I didn't want Beate to see that I'd broken it. She was sitting on the sofa. She looked at me. Good morning, she said. I nodded. She continued to look at me. Have we fallen out? she asked. No, I said. She kept her gaze fixed on me, I couldn't manage to read it. I sat down to get away from it. You misunderstood, I said. I didn't notice you getting up, I was lost in my own thoughts, and when I suddenly felt your hands on my neck, I mean, I see how it could make you . . . but I didn't know you were standing there. She didn't say anything. I looked at her, met the same inscrutable gaze. You have to believe me, I said. She looked away. Yes, she said, I do, don't I?

Sunhat

THEY SAT READING. Neither of them had spoken for a while, when she suddenly said: "When we go to Yugoslavia I'm going to get one of those sunhats I didn't buy myself last year."

"What page are you on?" he asked.

"Thirty-three. Why?"

"Just wondering."

She did not say any more and continued reading. For reasons he did not understand he found himself thinking about an exchange he had heard the previous night through the open window. First, a man's voice, from the street: "I couldn't be bothered flirting with you anymore." Then the voice of a woman, from a window (he thought): "Why not?" "I never get anywhere with it, do I?" That was it, not a word after that.

She was reading. He was sitting with his book open but was not reading; he looked at her. He thought: what was it that made her think of a sunhat?

After a while she put the book down.

"I'm going to fry an egg," she said. "Do you want one?"

"No, thanks." He didn't like fried eggs.

She went out to the kitchen and he picked up her book and turned to page thirty-three. He could find nothing there to account for the calling to mind of a sunhat or Yugoslavia. He thought: I can't figure her out, I thought I knew her, but I understand less and less about her. He decided to read all the pages preceding number thirty-three, maybe the answer lay there, but she came back in to fetch a cigarette, and he quickly put the book down again. Because he felt like a snoop and thought she had seen him looking at the book, he said:

"Is it an exciting read?"

"Exciting? Interesting."

"What's it about?"

"A person who wants something else . . . I don't know how to put it . . . someone who thinks she's doing fine but still longs for something. And she doesn't quite understand why, but sort of does, in a way. You know, the way people are."

"People?"

"Yes."

"I'm not that way."

"Well, you."

"Am I not people?"

"What do you mean by that? Oh, the egg!"

She began to hurry towards the kitchen, but turned, came back, and picked up the book.

He did not read any further. He thought: what did she mean by *well, you?* He tried to interpret the way she had said it but was unable. *I'm going to read that book,* he thought.

She returned, having eaten the fried egg in the kitchen; which struck him as unusual, she normally brought her evening snack into the sitting room.

He remarked upon it.

"Why did you eat in the kitchen?"

"What?"

"You ate in the kitchen," he said.

"Yeah?"

"You usually eat in here."

"Do I? No, I sometimes eat in the kitchen. What's with you? I eat in the kitchen all the time."

He didn't answer. He thought about it for a moment, but failed to see how that could be right. *I eat in the kitchen all the time.* That couldn't possibly be true.

"I think I'll go to bed," she said.

He looked at her but did not reply. She made eye contact, then in a calm, almost impassive tone said:

"I think I'm going mad."

"Oh?"

"I said I think I'm going mad."

"Maybe."

She looked at him, a hardness in her eyes, but only for a second.

"Maybe," she said.

He looked at her, coldly, and he was aware of it, even though he felt a hot unease within.

"Maybe," he repeated. "And what's brought on this madness?"

He saw her raise her shoulders. Then let them sink.

"Good night," she said. Then stood for a moment, before leaving.

He felt she had duped him and was withdrawing with a victory of sorts. He felt like he had been the loser and worked himself up. Bloody woman! he thought, what has she got into her head! Trying to make herself interesting, coming up with this insanity – her!

After a while he calmed down, but was not calm. He went to the kitchen and took a bottle of beer from the fridge. It was a quarter to ten. He returned to the living room, sat down, then got to his feet, and began pacing back and forth on the green carpet, pausing now and again to take a gulp of beer, while thinking conflicting thoughts. He thought: as if she has anything to complain about? And: she wants something else. *Someone who thinks she's doing fine but still longs for something else. You know, the way people are.*

One thing – due to whatever connotations she had in her head – had suddenly turned into something else entirely. Something harmless had become something complicated, serious. *I think I'm going mad.* She had meant that in one way or another, but in what way?

He fetched another beer, dismissed the idea she might have discovered something, about Anne, for instance, or Lucy. That was unlikely, she didn't know anyone in those circles, and he had taken every conceivable precaution.

He could not figure it out; he finished his drink and switched off the lights.

She was in bed reading. She barely glanced up before reimmersing herself in her book. He pretended nothing was wrong. He thought: she's acting as if nothing's wrong, fine by me, I won't go there.

He lay down, then turned his back to her as he switched off the lamp on the nightstand and said good night.

"Good night," she said.

He could not sleep. After a good while he became aware she was not turning the pages of the book. He lay listening to make sure. No, she was not turning them. Believing she had fallen asleep, he was about to stretch across to switch off the lamp on her nightstand but found she was lying with her eyes open looking at him over the top of the book. Her gaze was quite calm, yet there was something about it he found unsettling, something distant and simultaneously searching.

"Is my reading bothering you?" she asked. "Do you want me to turn out the light?"

"No, no," he replied. "I just thought . . . since you weren't reading."

"Yes I am. You can see that."

He jerked the book from her hand and looked at the page number. Thirty-eight. He gave it back, without saying anything.

"Why did you do that?" she said.

"You've read five pages since you went to fry an egg," he said.

"I'm thinking every now and then."

"I figured that much!"

"You remind me of my dad," she said.

He made no reply for a while, then said:

"I thought you liked him."

"Did you? Well I was fond of him."

What a thing to say, he thought, what the hell does she mean by that!

"Ha-ha!" he said, turning away from her.

"Dad was always playing God," she said. "If you know what I mean."

"No!" he said. "Nor am I interested! And now I'd like to go to sleep!"

"Of course, yes. Night-night."

Seething with anger, he suddenly got up, seized his duvet, pillow, and sheet and went to the living room, slamming the bedroom door behind him. He threw everything on the sofa, switched on the main light and strode purposefully out to the kitchen to fetch a bottle of beer. *You remind me of my dad. Dad was always playing God.*

Later, he went and took another bottle, and thought: I'm not going to the office tomorrow, will serve her right, she'll see the mess she's made.

Eventually he lay down, and eventually he slept.

He awoke with the sun in his face. For a moment or two he was disoriented, then he remembered everything.

He got up, walked quietly into the bedroom and got his clothes. She didn't wake up. He made a simple breakfast, then went out to the car and drove to the center of town. The electrical firm he was employed at had secured parking spaces for senior office staff on a demolition plot a few minutes walk away; it helped make the company a more attractive workplace.

He had a lot to do and didn't think very much about what had happened, but on the drive home, everything loomed so large that for a moment he considered punishing her by eating out. And although he thought it would certainly serve her right if he did, he decided that would only postpone matters and strengthen her hand. And he was not going to grant her that pleasure.

He let himself in, and all that met him was strikingly similar to what he usually encountered on coming home. She was friendly, and dinner – pork chops and stuffed cabbage – was ready. At first he was relieved, then he grew annoyed. Initially participating in the everyday chit-chat, then growing silent.

"Is there anything wrong?" she asked, but without concern, as though she might have asked: would you like more potatoes?

He decided not to answer. Then he said:

"No, why would there be?"

"I don't now, was just wondering."

Neither of them spoke after that. After eating, he went for a lie-down, as was his habit. What's the problem? he thought. I do love her after all.

He did not sleep, but lay down longer than usual. He could see no reason to get up.

She normally came in and woke him after a half hour so his afternoon nap did not affect his sleep at night. Today she did not.

After an hour he got up. She was not in the living room when he came in. A sheet of paper lay on the coffee table: "Just gone for a walk, Eva."

Oh, he thought, so she's suddenly just gone for a walk.

He was used to getting a coffee after his rest. He went out to the kitchen and put on the coffee maker.

He suddenly remembered the book. He wanted to read what she had read. He began to search for it, first in the living room, then in the bedroom, then finally the kitchen. He couldn't find it. He looked in drawers, behind the books on the bookshelf, in the kitchen cupboards, but without success.

He drank two cups of coffee. She did not come home.

He turned over the sheet of paper on the coffee table and wrote: "Just gone for a walk. Harry."

He went for a walk. He set out in the direction of the park, but changed his mind as there was a good chance Eva had gone there; she might think that he was looking for her.

He took a side street and headed north. After that he wandered aimlessly, thinking about himself, until finally arriving at the conclusion that he should have stayed at home; he would have been better off sitting on the sofa, looking composed when she arrived back.

He hurried home.

She was sitting on the sofa, looking composed. She glanced up from her book, smiled, then continued on reading. But it was a different book, he saw right away that it was much thicker than the one she had been reading the previous night.

He weighed up the cost of victory against defeat and decided he was going to take control of the situation. He turned on the cold-water tap, let the water run while studying his face, and thought: she has nothing to complain about – what the hell does she have to complain about! He turned off the tap and walked quickly into the living room. He said:

"If you've so much to complain about then you can just leave."

She looked at him, quizzically at first, then with that hard expression he had seen the night before.

"Leave? What do you mean by that?"

"If you're not happy with things, well then you can just go, can't you?"

"Oh? Can I? Go where?"

"Anywhere."

She put the book down, without closing it, but with the cover and back facing up, the way he had been taught not to lay down a book. Then she said:

"Why don't you sit down?"

"I'm fine standing, thank you."

"Please sit down, Harry."

He took a seat, looked down at his hands, and began scratching at his left thumbnail.

"We need to talk," she said.

He did not reply.

"Can't we talk together," she said.

"Talk away."

"Talk *together*, Harry."

He scratched at his thumbnail.

"I feel isolated, Harry. I know what we agreed, but it . . . back then I didn't know what staying at home all day would mean. Don't get me wrong, I've nothing against the things I do, but it's not enough, and well . . . I'm stuck here all day long feeling . . . So, this morning I applied for a job, and it's mine if I want it, I've said yes, but I can of course change my mind, but I told them I can start at the beginning of the month."

There was a long silence, then he said:

"I see."

"I think I have to take that job, Harry."

"Oh? In other words I've no say in the matter."

"You don't understand. You're going to be happy about it too."

"I just don't know what's in my own best interests, is that what you mean?"

"You don't know how I feel."

"You think you're going mad."

Her tone of voice, no longer intended to be persuasive, took on a harsh, cold timbre that left him perplexed when she said:

"Don't you dare not take me seriously! Don't you dare!"

He realized he had gone too far, but was incapable of admitting it, so he said nothing, but suddenly felt extremely uneasy and insecure.

There was a long silence. He glanced at her; the last thing she had said still showed in her face, her expression simultaneously aggressive yet impassive.

"What kind of job is it?" he eventually asked.

"At the department store." Her tone was cold, implacable. "In the kitchenware section."

Most of the customers there *would* be women, he thought.

"This is all very sudden," he said. "And we did have an agreement, after all."

"I'm aware of that. But that was then. Besides, you said that most of my earnings would be eaten up by tax."

"And you thought keeping house couldn't be anything but wonderful."

"Yes. I did. We were wrong, both of us."

"We're not going to be much better off, if that's what you think."

"We won't be any worse off, at least."

She spoke as if she knew and he did not pursue the issue. All in all she spoke differently, the aspect of semi-inquiry behind her words, which he was accustomed to and liked so much, was gone.

He was hit by the realization he had lost. He could not prevent her from doing what she wanted. He had a choice between being defied or of being accommodating in such a way so as to not suffer defeat.

He thought for a moment, then rose to his feet and said:

"Do you want a beer?"

"Now? No, thanks."

He returned from the kitchen, placed the glass and the beer bottle down on the coffee table, but remained standing.

"I can see now that this means a lot to you, and you do know that I've always had your best interests at heart, even though I may not always have been able to see what really was in your best interests."

"But still more able than me?" she interjected.

He did not understand what she meant, but he found the impatience with which she said it hurtful. Here he was, about to grant her her wish, and she cut him short like that!

He shrugged resignedly, then poured the beer into the glass, but remained standing.

"Sorry," she said. "I interrupted you."

He took a drink.

"Be that as it may," he said, "what I was intending to say was that I think you should take the job, although you're probably planning to do that, regardless of what I think."

He met her gaze, she had a strange look in her eyes, and he was unable to interpret it. He looked away and took a swig from his glass. Then he waited, but she did not say anything. He waited and waited, took another gulp, emptying the glass, before filling it up again.

Finally, with her eyes fixed on her lap, in a tone of voice he was still unable to interpret – it sounded so flat, as though the words were coming from far away or almost as if from out of nowhere – she said:

"Of course, you know I wouldn't do it if you didn't think it was right."

The Grasshopper

MARIA MADE an inappropriate remark about him in front of the others; it peeved him. He did his best to seem unperturbed, but when the guests had gone, and Maria said she was tired, he opened another bottle of wine and put a log on the fire. Aren't you coming to bed? she asked. He replied that he wasn't tired and felt like another drink. She looked at him. Tomorrow's another day, she said. I'm aware of that, he said, and that was the only hint of aggression he managed to express.

He stayed up for an hour. He drank two glasses of wine. Then he took the bottle into the kitchen and emptied most of the wine into the sink. He brought the bottle back out and placed it beside the empty glass.

He woke up late the next day and he was alone in bed. He got up right away. The house was empty but the table was set for breakfast – but just for him. The coffee in the thermos was lukewarm. He drank two cups. The Sunday paper lay beside the plate. He picked it up and went out onto the veranda. Maria was on her knees in the vegetable garden, almost hidden behind the dahlias; he pretended not to see her and sat down with his back to her. He opened the paper and sat looking over the top of it: some treetops, a pale blue sky. He sat like that until he heard footsteps on the gravel and her voice behind him: Good morning. He lowered the paper and looked at her. Good morning, he said. She pulled off her gardening gloves and came up the steps. Did you stay up long? A couple of hours, he said. That long? she said. He folded the paper, without replying, and then he said: I was thinking about paying Dad a visit. But I've invited Vera to lunch, she said. I'll be back by then, he said. You won't make it, she said. So we'll eat an hour later then, he said. Just because you suddenly decide that you want to visit your father? He did not reply. She went inside. He got up and went in after her to get his coat. You haven't even eaten, she said. I'm not hungry, he said. He met her gaze; she studied him. What's the matter with you, she said. Nothing, he said.

Later on, as he was driving out of town in the direction of R, he felt almost cocky, and he thought: I do as I please.

Halfway to R he left the motorway and drove toward the end of the Bu fjord. There was a small outdoor café there, and he bought two sandwiches and a coffee. He sat under a tree and looked out over the fjord. He lit up a cigarette. Now and then he checked his watch. He smoked two more cigarettes, then got to his feet and walked slowly back to the car.

He drove the same way back and arrived home before they had sat down to eat. Maria asked how his father was, and he said: He didn't recognize me. Vera said it must be difficult seeing your father so utterly helpless. He nodded. They sat down to eat. He poured them red wine. They ate roast beef. They talked about everyday things, he offered the odd yes and no in agreement; his thoughts were often elsewhere, but he made sure the whole time that the wine glasses were never empty. And when, toward the end of the meal, Maria wanted to hear more about his father's condition, her questions collided with an aggressive thought he had just had, and his reply was rather rash and dismissive: You're suddenly very interested in my father. There was silence. Then, in a low voice, Vera said: That wasn't a very nice thing to say, Jakob. No, he answered, almost as quietly, but it's got nothing to do with you. He took hold of his glass, his hand trembling. I think you ought to explain yourself, said Maria. He didn't reply. I don't know what to think, she said. He leaned back in his chair and looked at her. He said: Dad is fine. He doesn't know what's going on around him anymore, but if the nurses are kind to him, then he's in safe hands. So he's fine. It grew quiet again, then Maria said: You could have just said that straight off. There are a lot of things that could be said straight off, he said. What do you mean by that? she said. Do I mean something by it? he said. Really, she said, now you're just being impossible. She stood up and began to clear the table, and when Vera got up as well, she said: No, no, just sit down. Jakob saw Vera hesitate, then she picked up the vegetable bowl and the gravy boat and followed Maria into the kitchen. Jakob poured himself some wine, then got to his feet, picked up his glass and went out onto the veranda. He smoked a cigarette, then he smoked one more. His glass was soon empty. Vera came out. She sat down. What a summer, she said. Yes, he said. But actually, she said, August is quite . . . there's something wistful about it, don't you think, like it's the end of something. He looked at her, did not reply. As a child, she said, I always associated August, especially the evenings, with grasshoppers, their chirping, I thought it was so nice. Now there are no grasshoppers anymore. Aren't there? he said. No, she said. He looked at her; she was sitting with her head lowered, examining a fingernail. He said: Would you like some wine? Yes, please, she said. He went in and fetched a bottle and a glass. Maria was not there. Vera was sitting in the same position, as though lost in thought, and when he had filled her glass, then his own, he stood looking down at her for a moment and a sudden warmth passed through him, like a jolt, and he said: You look so pretty. Me? she said. He did not reply, just sat down. There was silence for a while. Then she said: It's a long time since anyone has said that. Can I have a cigarette? He held the pack out to her. I didn't know you smoked, he said. No, she said, I've quit. He gave her a light. From the doorway, Maria said: Oh Vera, really. I know, said Vera. Has Jakob led you astray? Vera looked at Jakob and said: Yes, in a way. But I made up my own mind to follow him. Maria came out onto the veranda, pulled a chair over to the table and sat down. Jakob asked if he should get her a glass, he felt light and free. He fetched the glass and poured some wine into it. Vera blew smoke rings. Look, she said, I can still do it. You're playing with fire, Maria said. Yes, Vera said, I'd almost forgotten how good it was. I told you, said Maria. Vera blew more rings up into the almost still air. You're putting your willpower to the test now, said Maria. Spare me, said Vera. She looked at Jakob and added: Maria's never quite got over being the big sister. I can see that, he said. Rubbish, Maria said. Maria doesn't play with fire, Jakob said. Oh, I'm sure she does, Vera said, isn't that right, Maria? Everyone does. Maria sipped at her glass. Could well be, she said, but I avoid getting burned. Jakob laughed. Maria looked at him. Vera put out the cigarette. It's humid, said Maria. Yes, said Vera. Imagine if there was a real thunderstorm. And a bolt of lightning struck that ugly house over there. Oh, Vera, really, Maria said. Jakob laughed. Do you think that's funny? Maria said. Yes, said Jakob, that's why I laughed. It was completely quiet, for a long time, then Maria got to her feet. She stood for a moment, then walked to the steps and down into the garden. Say something, said Vera. He did not reply. He poured wine into her glass. I'm getting tipsy, she said. And why not, he said, that's what wine's for. I think I'll be off, she said. I'd like it if you stayed, he said. I'll just turn naughty, she said. So do, he said. Naughty girl, she said, looking at him. He looked away but could feel she was still looking at him. Are you getting nervous now? she said. Not nervous, he said. What then? she said. Maria came across the lawn. The carrots are bumping into one another, she said. Bumping? Jakob said. They need to be thinned, she said. She came up the steps and placed three small tomatoes on the table. Taste how good they are, she said. Vera picked one up. I think I'll find myself a man with a garden as well, she said.

Yes, why not? said Maria. And a veranda like this, said Vera, where you can sit even when it's raining. We never sit here when it rains, Maria said. Of course we do, Jakob said. I often sit here when it rains. You do not, said Maria. I certainly do, said Jakob. I would have sat here in any case, Vera said. She put the tomato in her mouth. Along with my husband, she said. What husband? Maria said. The one with the garden and the veranda, said Vera. You're tipsy, said Maria. Yes, indeed, said Vera. I'll make some coffee, said Maria. She went inside. Vera took a large gulp of wine. Coffee! she said. Jakob filled up her glass. Thanks, she said. And a cigarette, if you have one. He gave her a cigarette and a light. Is it true you sit here when it's raining? she said. On occasion, he said, but it's been a long time since I have. So it wasn't true then, she said. No, he said, but there was no way Maria could know that. But you made her out to be a liar, she said. No more than she made me out to be a liar by saying that I haven't sat here. But that's the truth, Vera said. Yes, but she doesn't know that. Maybe she knows it because she knows you, said Vera. She doesn't know me, Jakob said. Maria came out and put down three cups. She looked at Vera but didn't say anything. She went back inside. Poor Maria, said Vera. Jakob did not reply. I'm going to have a coffee and then I'll be off, she said. He did not reply. She put out the cigarette. Maria brought the coffee, poured it into the cups and sat down. Jakob got up and walked into the living room, down the hall, and out onto the street; he stood for a moment, then he set off toward the center of town.

He came home two hours later. Vera and Maria were sitting in the living room; they still had not switched on the lights. There you are, said Maria. Yes, he said. We were just sitting here wondering where you'd got to, said Maria. I had to buy cigarettes, he said. It was completely quiet for a time, then he said: It's getting cloudy. Yes, Maria said, we saw that. We heard a grasshopper, said Vera. Oh? Jakob said. He glanced at her; she looked away. He took the cigarette pack out of his pocket. Would you like one? he said. No thanks, said Vera. I've quit again. He lit one for himself. Anyone care for a beer? he said. They did not. He went to the kitchen and fetched a bottle, took a glass, came back, and sat down. Nobody spoke. Well, I'd better be off, Vera said. You're welcome to stay the night, said Maria. I won't, but thanks, said Vera. After all, there's no one waiting for you, said Maria. No, come to think of it, there isn't, said Vera. I don't have anyone waiting up for me. You make it sound like you feel sorry for me. Nonsense, said Maria, nobody feels sorry for you, why would anyone feel sorry for you? No, that's what I'm saying, said Vera, so don't ask me to stay because no one's waiting for me. I could just as well stay even if someone were waiting for me. Yes, of course, said Maria. Vera got up. Are you leaving? said Maria. I'm going to the toilet, said Vera. Jakob followed her with his eyes. She's so difficult, said Maria. Jakob did not reply. Maria stood up and switched on the floor lamp. And you just disappeared, she said. He did not reply. She stood beside the light; he didn't look at her. He heard her breathing was fast and heavy, then she said: I can't take this much longer. Right, he said. Is that all you've got to say, she said. He did not reply. Oh Christ, she said. Jakob heard Vera coming down the stairs. Maria switched off the light and sat down. The room was almost dark. Vera came into the living room, went over to the open veranda door, and stood looking out. Jakob got to his feet. I should be getting off before it starts to rain, said Vera. Jakob walked down the hall and into the guestroom. He closed the door. The bed was made. He stood for a few moments looking at it and felt a quiver run through him. Then he went to the window. The cloud bank had drawn very close; it split the sky in two. He pulled a chair over. He sat with his elbows resting on the windowsill looking out at the dusk. After a while he heard low voices coming from the hall, then the door being opened, then it went quiet. He did not move. Suddenly a wind swept through the leaves of the tree outside the window, and a few moments later the rain came. She didn't make it, he thought. He tried to detect sounds in the house, but heard only the rain. It had grown almost completely dark. And all at once it went bright, and a few seconds later distant thunder could be heard. Maria will be scared now, he thought. There was more lightning and more thunder; he counted the seconds; the intervals grew shorter and shorter. She's scared now, he thought. He got up and went to the door, opened it slightly, and listened. He stood like that for a while, then he went down the hall into the living room. Maria was not there. He went back out and up the stairs, into the bedroom. She was lying with the duvet over her head. Maria, he said. She pulled the duvet aside. She was fully dressed. I was so scared, she said. There's nothing to be scared of, he said. I thought you'd left, she said. He went over to the window. Don't stand there, she said, please. He saw her reflection in the pane. It's not dangerous, he said, we have lightning rods. I know, she said, but it scares me, and it scares me even more when you stand there. He took a couple of steps back; he could still see her. She got out of bed. Looks like it's over now, he said. I thought you had gone, she said. Where would I have gone, he said.

.

The Joker

ONE SATURDAY EVENING in late November I was at home alone with Lucy. I was sitting in the chair by the window, she was at the dining table playing patience, she'd been playing it constantly of late, I didn't know why but figured perhaps she was worried about something. It's so hot, she said, could you open the window a little. I agreed that it was rather warm, and moreover unseasonably mild out, so I opened it. The window faced the back garden and a small copse and I stood for a few moments listening to the rain falling softly. Maybe that was the reason, the soft rainfall and the silence, in any case what can occasionally occur did occur: that great emptiness descended, as though the very meaninglessness of existence creeps inside and unfolds within like an endless bare landscape. You can close it now, Lucy said, even though I was still standing looking out. I'm going to take a little walk, I said. Now? she said. I closed the window. Just a short stroll, I said. She continued playing patience without looking up. I went into the hall and put on the raincoat and sou'wester I usually only wear while gardening in bad weather. Maybe that's the reason I went out to the garden instead of onto the road. I walked right to the end, where we grew winter cabbage and there was a short bench without a backrest that had been there since Lucy inherited the house. I sat in the rain and darkness looking up at the light from the windows, but due to the downward slope of the garden I couldn't see Lucy, just the ceiling and the topmost part of the walls. After a while it grew too chilly to sit still; I got to my feet, intending to climb over the fence, walk through the copse and out onto the road by the post office. But on reaching the fence I turned, and that was when I saw Lucy's shadow on the inside wall and a small part of the ceiling, and I couldn't understand how that could be, where a light that could cause her shadow to fall there could be coming from. I climbed up onto the fence where it was possible to hold on to the bottom branch of a large oak tree; I balanced on the fence, stood up straight, and saw Lucy by the table, a candle burning in front of her, holding something in one hand that was also aflame, although it was impossible to see what. Then the flame went out, and Lucy stood up; as she did so it was as though the entire room fell into shadow. The next moment she'd disappeared from view. I waited a while but she didn't return. I jumped down on the other side of the fence and went into the copse, I wondered what she had burned, I felt hoodwinked, I know that's exactly how I felt because I pondered the thought, even wondered where the expression 'hoodwinked' came from. I followed the path until I came out on the gravel car park behind the post office, where I stopped and weighed up my options, then walked back the same way, which wasn't far, only a couple of hundred meters, and then I arrived back at the fence.

I took my time in the hall, and when I came in she was playing patience again. She looked up from the cards and sent me a little smile. There was no candle on the table and no remnants of burnt paper in the ashtray. Well? she said. It's raining, I replied. You already knew that, she said. Yes, I answered. I sat down by the window. I looked out at the garden but saw only the reflection of the room and of Lucy. After a while, without looking up from the cards and in a quite normal tone of voice, she said: I only need to pinch myself to know that I exist. This statement was brief and to the point, even for Lucy, and when I wholly perceived it as an accusation, I ascribe that to the feeling I had of being hoodwinked, a feeling not lessened on my returning to find all traces of what I had seen from the garden fence erased. I was on the verge of a sarcastic reply but bit my tongue. I said nothing, didn't even turn my head, but continued gazing at her reflection in the windowpane. She began gathering the cards, but still did not look up. I felt quite stony-faced. She put the deck of cards in the box and stood up, slowly. She looked at me. I couldn't turn around, I was completely fixed in my own aggrievement. She said: Poor you, Joachim. Then she left. I heard her turn on the tap in the kitchen, followed by the sound of the bedroom door closing, then it went quiet. I don't know how long I sat bitterly chewing on her last words, several minutes perhaps, but eventually my thoughts took another direction. I got up and went over to the fire-place. It was just as empty of ashes as it had been earlier in the day. I wanted to go to the kitchen and check the rubbish bin, but the thought of Lucy unexpectedly walking in gave me pause. So what if she did? I said to myself, after all, she doesn't know that I saw her. I opened the cupboard door below the sink and atop the rubbish in the bin lay the charred corner of a playing card. I picked it up, turned it this way and that, confused and at a loss. The questions jumbled in my mind: had she gone and fetched a candle to set a card alight? One of the same cards she'd been playing patience with? Why a candle? Why burn a card? Why had she put the candle back where it was? Which card? I might be able to find an answer to the last question; I dropped the burnt remains of the card back into the bin and went to the living room. The pack of cards lay on the table, I took out the deck and counted them, fifty-three. There was only one joker. She had burned a joker. I looked at the one that was still intact: a winking jester producing an ace of hearts from up his sleeve. I slipped the card into my pocket with a vague feeling of getting even, then put the deck back in the box.

When I went to bed an hour later, Lucy was asleep. I lay awake for a long time, and the next morning I remembered everything. It was rain-ing. I tried to act as though it were a normal Sunday morning but wasn't able. We ate breakfast in silence, that is to say, Lucy made a couple of mundane remarks but I made no reply. Then she said: You don't have to sit there saying nothing for my sake. At this I saw red. I was sitting with a knife in my hand and I brought the handle so hard down on the plate that it cracked. Then I stood up and on my way out of the room I shouted: Poor you, Joachim, poor you, Joachim!

I returned home several hours later. I'd planned on saying that I was sorry for being unable to control myself. The entire house lay in darkness. I switched on the lights. There was a sheet of paper on the kitchen table that said: *Okay. I'll call you tomorrow or another day. Lucy*

That was how she went out of my life. After eight years. At first I refused to believe it, I was certain that once she had a little time she'd realize she needed me just as much as I needed her. But I now know she didn't realize that, and just have to accept it, she wasn't the person I thought she was.

The Nail in the Cherry Tree

MOM WAS STANDING in the small back garden, a long time ago now, I was a lot younger then. She was hammering a long nail into the trunk of the cherry tree, I saw her from the second-storey window, it was a humid, overcast day in August, I saw her hang the hammer up on the long nail, before walking to the wooden fence at the end of the garden where she stood, quite motionless, looking out over the extended treeless plain, for a long time. I walked downstairs and out into the garden, I didn't like her just standing there, there was no telling what she'd see. I went over and stood beside her. She touched my arm, looked up at me and smiled. She had been crying. She smiled and said: I can't take it, Nicolay. No, I said. We walked up to the house and into the kitchen, and just then Sam arrived. He complained about the heat, and Mom put on the kettle. The windows were open. Sam was telling Mom about a bed that was giving his wife a sore back, and I went upstairs, up to Sam's room, as it was called, since he was the eldest and the first one to have his own room. I stood in the middle of Sam's room letting time pass, and then I went back down. Sam was talking about an outboard engine. Mom put some sugar in her tea and stirred and stirred with the spoon. Sam wiped his neck with a blue handkerchief, I couldn't stand to look at him, I told Mom I was off to buy tobacco, and I took my time, but when I got back he was still sitting there. He was talking about the funeral, about how the priest had found just the right words. You think? Mom said. I asked Sam how old his son was. He looked at me. Seven, he said, you know that. I didn't answer, he continued looking at me, and Mom got up and brought the cups to the sink. So he'll be starting school, I said. Of course, he said, everyone starts school when they're seven. Yes, I replied, I know. I got up and walked into the hall, up the stairs and into Sam's room, my head felt like it was at the bottom of a lake. I put the tobacco pouch into my suitcase, locked it and pocketed the key. No, I said to myself. I opened the suitcase again, took out the tobacco pouch, took the other pouch out of my pocket, and walked down to the kitchen with both of them in my hand. Sam stopped talking. Mom was drying the dishes with a red-check tea towel. I sat down, put both pouches on the table, and rolled a cigarette. Sam looked at me. There was silence for a long time, then Mom began to hum. What about you, Sam said, you're still at the same thing? Yes, I said. I'll never get it, he said. Grown men writing poetry. Not doing anything else, I mean. Now, now, Sam, Mom said. But I don't get it, Sam said. That's understandable, I said. I got up and went out to the garden. It was too small for me, I climbed over the fence and began walking across the plain. I wanted to be visible, but from a distance. I walked about eighty, ninety, maybe one hundred meters, then came to a halt and turned around. I could see half of Sam's car to the right of the house. The air was quite still. I hardly felt a thing. I stood looking at the house and the car for a long time, maybe a quarter of an hour, maybe longer, until Sam drove away, I didn't see him, only the car. Mom came out into the garden immediately after, and when I saw that she'd seen me, I walked back. She said Sam had to be off, he said to give you his regards. You don't say, I said. He is your brother, she said. Ah Mom, I said. She shook her head and smiled. I asked if she wanted to have a rest, and she did. We went in. She stopped in the middle of the room. She opened her mouth wide, as if she wanted to scream, or as though she needed air, then she closed it again and said in a feeble voice: I don't think I can get over it, Nicolay. I just want to die. I put my arms around her frail, bony shoulders. Mom, I said. I just want to die, she repeated. Yes, Mom, I said. I led her to the sofa, she was crying, I laid the blanket over her legs, her eyes were squeezed shut and she wept loudly, I sat on the edge of the sofa, looked at the tears and thought of Dad, that she must have loved him. I placed my hand on her bosom, in a way I was aware of what I was doing, and she stopped squeezing her eyes, but didn't open them. Oh Nicolay, she said. Sleep, Mom, I said. I didn't take my hand away. After a while, her breathing was steady, and I got up, went into the hall, up the stairs and into Sam's room. The train wasn't leaving for almost five hours, but I was sure she would understand. I packed my suitcase, putting the black suit in last. My head felt like it was in a large room. I went down the stairs and out the door. I walked the whole way to the station, it was quite far, but I had plenty of time. I walked along thinking that she must have loved Dad, and that Sam . . . that she probably loved him too. And I thought: it doesn't matter.

The Other Dream

I CAME OUTSIDE one day and saw they had torn down the house next door. I hadn't noticed anything, but then fortunately I'm hard of hearing. It was a strange spectacle, even with my poor eyesight. It had been a big house with many rooms, now all the rooms were gone, reduced to a surprisingly modest pile of bricks and splintered wood.

The empty space so surprised and preoccupied me that I became sidetracked and forgot why I had gone out, so I went back inside.

I took the stairs. It was good to have a sit down afterwards; sometimes your efforts are rewarded: I fell asleep. It's a pleasant state, although often too short-lived.

As was the case this time.

I think I hear somebody place a hand on the doorknob, but I can't be sure, my partial deafness often leads me to imagine things.

Then there's a knock at the door.

At first I pretend to think it's the usual dream, not the other one.

But then there's a second knock.

I don't want to open. I got over feeling guilty about letting people go away empty-handed long ago. I remain sitting perfectly still in the chair for a long time.

Then there's a third knock.

Now I can't possibly open, whether I want to or not. Even so, I have to admit, I grow a little anxious.

Forced by this feeling of unease, I get up quietly and move towards the hall, but before getting too far I hear the door opening. I know it was locked.

I hurry to sit back down.

I'm afraid.

I have no defense against physical force. I close my eyes and pretend to be asleep; God knows where that idea came from. I hear footsteps. They come closer. Then stop.

I don't open my eyes, I want to give him time, and thus avoid him doing anything rash.

I can feel the quivering of my eyelids and the pounding of my blood.

After the Funeral Service

M Y BROTHER'S FUNERAL service took place on March 6th. It was
a Tuesday. He'd been dead nine days by then. That's far too long,
I think.

It had rained a little every day but on Tuesday morning the sky was
blue. I called up Maria to say I wasn't going, that I'd fallen ill.

Maria's my sister. She didn't believe me. At first she said I was being
a coward, then she began to beg and plead.

For my sake, she said, please.

I didn't answer. I heard her crying.

Are you crying? I asked.

Please, she said, I can't take any more.

Then I told her I'd go after all.

The funeral service was at eleven. I've attended four burials or crema-
tions before but never so early in the day. I was at Father's, because he
died before Mother, and I went to that for Mother's sake. I wasn't at
my mother's, she was dead after all. I couldn't take it, I loved her so
very much.

So why should I attend Karl's – for Maria's sake, I suppose. I am quite fond of her as well.

So I went.

There were four men standing outside the small chapel. I only saw them from a distance. I looked down as I walked past them, and continued looking down as I made my way between the rows of benches to the front, knowing that was where the next of kin sit.

Maria had kept a place for me. I sat between her and Henriette, Mother's sister. She took my hand and held it awhile. She's over seventy years old.

Maria's two children were sitting on her other side, as was their father, that is to say Maria's husband. He's a shopkeeper. The children do not resemble either of them, perhaps because Maria and her husband, Kristian, are so different. Neither do the two children resemble one another. Personally, I would have preferred to resemble Mother, but I don't.

A few minutes passed, then a low deep tone came from the organ, followed by some notes of a higher pitch that lay on top of the deeper one. It was so beautiful, and I pictured a large, placid lake surrounded by green trees. Then the sound began to swell, rippling the surface of the water and bending the trees in the wind. The priest was rather young. He was dark-haired and had a high-pitched voice. He spoke about Karl as though he knew him. He talked about the seemingly chance events leading to Karl being where he was at that exact time, and how that also went for the man in the oncoming car. He didn't elaborate on why he'd said *seemingly,* even though that had to be the word that was supposed to give the sentence meaning.

It wasn't a particularly good speech and nobody took to tears, not even when he said that we, the bereaved, must not hold in our inevitable, life-giving grief.

They were the exact words he used. I didn't understand them, which is why I remember.

It was easier, in a sense, to leave the chapel than it had been to enter, even though those of us on the front row of benches went first, which meant the people sitting behind had a good view of us. Perhaps it was due to the organ music.

I walked beside Henriette. She had wanted to be alongside me. She's twice as old as me. She lives just fifty meters from where I do. I live on the third floor of an old apartment building, she's on the first floor of a neighboring block, only a parking lot, a wire fence, and some rather high linden trees separate the two buildings. In autumn and winter, as well as early spring, before any leaves appear on the trees, I can see her when she's standing by the cooker or sitting at the kitchen table. She's aware of that, I told her once, and she said: That's nice to know.

When we emerged into the harsh light all I wanted to do was get away, so I told Henriette I'd like to go to Mother's grave.

May I join you? she asked.

We walked along the side of the chapel and past the church. The graveyard is situated on a south-facing slope between tall, straight pine trees that cast large shadows.

Are you often here? Henriette asked.

No, I said, are you?

No, she replied.

As we stood by the grave, Henriette said: I suppose this is where Karl will be laid to rest now.

Did Maria say that? I asked.

No, but it would be only natural. It is a family plot after all.

I don't want to be buried here, I said.

You don't?

Do you want to be buried here? I asked.

I don't know. Do you think I should be?

I made no reply. Then I said: You were very fond of Mother, weren't you?

Oh yes. I loved her very much.

Do you think they're gone now? I asked.

I can't see them, she said, but if you want we can go through the gate at the bottom of the graveyard.

Georg

I'D KNOWN GEORG in passing, from about four or five years back. I was sitting by myself sober, with a beer. He walked over from another table and sat down without asking. He did however ask if I could buy him a beer.

No, I said.

He ordered one all the same.

You're on a bender, I said.

For the last four months, he replied.

I didn't say anything. He said I was a decent sort.

Sure, I said.

You know why? he said.

No, I said.

Doesn't make any difference, he said.

He asked again if I could stand him a beer.

No, I said.

The waiter arrived with the beer. Georg paid. Then he picked up my tobacco pouch and tried to roll a cigarette. He couldn't manage and it ended up all over the tablecloth so I rolled one for him.

While I was doing that, he asked me what went through my mind when I woke up one day and it was all over, and I lay in bed and knew it was all over, and just lay there, longing for her to come back, what went through my head then?

Felt sorry for myself, I said.

You're honest, he said.

I made no reply.

Am I in the way? he asked.

Of what? I said.

Good one, he said, good one.

I didn't say anything; I thought: best to leave.

Seen Inger at all?

Inger? I said.

The woman you were married to, for fuck's sake!

No, I said, not for about six months.

Can I ask you something? he said. You don't have to answer but can I ask you something?

Ask away, I said.

You've always been so damned good at talking, he said, you always say the right things and forever have some clever answer at the ready. But there were times, when you were still together with Inger, that she'd come over and ask me if I thought you meant what you said.

And? I said.

No, that was it.

You were going to ask me something, I said.

I have asked, he said, don't you get it?

Will you buy me a beer? he said.

No, I said.

He signaled to the waiter and ordered a beer. Then he said: She asked me if I thought you meant what you said.

I hope so, I said.

You're real fucking smart all right, he said.

Why don't you go find yourself another table, I said.

He remained seated, staring intently at me. I didn't want him to see that it bothered me. I rolled a cigarette.

I can see right through you, he said.

Can you? I said.

I lit up the cigarette and pocketed the tobacco pouch, along with the lighter. I looked around but I could feel him staring.

I see now why she became such a slut after she left you, he said.

I blew smoke in his face.

The waiter came with the beer; Georg paid.

I continued to blow smoke in his face.

He said: Quit doing that.

I continued.

Fine, he said, well, suddenly you seem to have run out of all your words. Well, that's just fine, means you won't be able to fool people anymore, but that's okay, blow your smoke, go ahead.

He leaned back in the chair to get away from the smoke.

I continued to blow it.

To think you used to be such a wiseass, and now all you can do with your mouth is blow smoke out of it. But that's okay, I'm leaving.

He rose from the chair.

I put the cigarette out and drained my glass.

He remained standing.

Weren't you going? I said.

He didn't reply. Then he said: I'm not the one who should be fucking leaving.

I signaled to the waiter for another beer. I could feel my heart pounding. I took the lighter and the pouch of tobacco from my pocket and rolled a fresh cigarette.

Gerhard P

A COUPLE OF weeks after Gerhard P, at the age of forty-three, lost his parents in a car accident, a sense of calm descended upon him that he did not understand and that at certain moments left him feeling slightly guilty.

He was the sole beneficiary of the will, and as he had taken for granted he would outlive his parents, he had often dreamed of at some point taking over his childhood home – a spacious detached residence on the outskirts of the city. Now the house was his and before a month had passed he moved in.

It was a Friday in early December, a light snow was falling and dusk was gathering.

When the removal men left, he switched off the lights and undressed, then walked naked from room to room, whether heated or not, and on entering each one, he said: here I am.

He put the most feeling into this statement when standing in his parents' bedroom. The large marital bed was unmade; it had been left as it was since that afternoon they had set out in the car and drove eastward, for an uncertain purpose and destination. They had only made it thirty kilometers; at which point his father came over into the oncoming lane and collided head-on with an articulated lorry.

Gerhard stood naked in the middle of the room and, with his eyes fixed on the unmade bed, said in a low voice: here I am.

Then he went down to the living room, got dressed and switched on the light.

Later, after eating a simple meal, Gerhard set about rearranging the furniture, starting with the living room. Nothing was to remain as it was.

He had figured out beforehand how he wanted it, but after a while he realized his plan was not feasible and he pushed the furniture back into place.

He fetched one of the wine bottles his parents had left, poured himself a glass, sat down in the sofa and looked around. Everything was the same way he seemed to recall it had always been.

He thought: here I am.

Gustav Herre

GUSTAV HERRE STOOD by the window looking down at the street below; he often did, although there wasn't much to see – it was a quiet street in a quiet part of town. He looked toward the windows opposite also, but with his head bowed, so that the neighbors across the way would not take him for a Peeping Tom.

He had never seen anything of consequence, neither behind the windows nor on the street. And what he saw on this September afternoon, at around four o'clock, was itself highly inconsequential: a dark-skinned man in his sixties, with a slight stoop, who was lame in one leg, a defect that made him easy to recognize. Gustav Herre had seen him before, from his third-storey window, but without it giving rise to any reaction or reflection.

He viewed himself, with some satisfaction, as a dispassionate man, and his reaction now, although not strong, surprised him. He thought: poor man, so far away from where he would rather be, so far from his country, its landscape and language.

Gustav Herre watched the man until he disappeared from view by the hairdresser's on the corner, then returned to his desk further into the room to continue work on his essay "Modernism as Liberation and Pretext." He sat looking at what he had already written and soon realized he was not going to get much more work done today after all.

He checked his watch; to his mild irritation, he found he was already waiting for the woman who had called earlier that day and said she could come over if he wanted her to.

A few hours later she was there, in his bed. He lay awhile looking at her – at her forehead, hair, one visible ear, cheek, and nose. She had closed her eyes. Then he got up and covered her with the duvet.

Do you feel like shrimp? he said.

Lovely, she said.

He set the table, put out the shrimp, bread, butter, mayonnaise and a bottle of white wine. He drank a glass of brandy.

She came out of the bathroom and told him she could not stay late because her husband would be back early the next morning. Gustav Herre said that that was mean of him.

Yes, she said.

She asked if he was jealous.

No, he said, should I be?

She made no reply.

They sat down at the table. He filled their glasses. They ate shrimp and drank wine. Gustav Herre apologized that there was no roe in the shrimp, however she actually preferred that.

Gradually the wine enlivened them. She mentioned, in relation to something or other, how she sometimes derived satisfaction from throwing away chocolate wrappers or the like on the sidewalk; The funny thing is, she said, it gives me a bad conscience.

Gustav Herre viewed that as quite natural, after all she obviously did it in order to be disobedient; In our world, he said, throwing away paper on the street on purpose was an immoral act and a protest against the established order.

She laughed.

That's a bit lofty, she said.

Gustav Herre poured more wine into the glasses.

Aesthetics elevates or reduces to morality, he said, an empty cigarette packet or an empty cola can on a pavement; all of a sudden what is otherwise acceptable becomes unacceptable because it's in the wrong place.

I've always been interested in that, he continued, when I was around nineteen or twenty I went through a phase of planting different objects in places where they didn't belong.

He laughed.

It started, he said, when he came across an old broken frame in the attic, the kind one put family photos in. The glass was intact and when he had made a reasonable job of fixing the frame, he placed a picture in it, which he had cut out of a magazine or periodical; it was a detail from an old painting, probably from the 17th century; it showed an old couple, both blind, welcoming home their son, who was also blind, and the father was biting the son on the cheek.

Or something like that, he said, he could not remember exactly, but it was a powerful, distressing image that he had had his reasons for liking.

Then he had taken the picture to one of the forests outside of town and nailed it up on a tree trunk some fifteen or twenty meters from the trail.

Why? she said.

So that someone would find it and not understand why it was hanging there, Gustav Herre said: Jesus, I was young . . .

He poured wine into their glasses while he searched for something to say.

What a stupid story, she said.

Yes, he said.

Konrad T

O N TUESDAY, KONRAD T visited his father. He had been doing so ever since moving back to the capital after the breakup of a long-term relationship. He took no pleasure in calling on him but did so; he could not bring himself not to.

On this particular Tuesday Konrad was running late. Less than a half hour before he was due to leave, a relatively recent acquaintance, Vibeke, dropped by. He told her she should have phoned in advance. She said she had acted on impulse, having had an errand nearby. She kissed him. His relationship with her was unclear; he seldom missed her when she wasn't around but her physical presence almost unfailingly aroused his desire, due in no small part to the change that came over her when she was feeling amorous: from being a woman who was composed and proper, she became quite uninhibited, in both what she said and did.

They had slept together.

This led to his arriving a half hour late. He made up an excuse. His father could not tell he was lying by looking at him. He was blind. Some few years previously he had got cataracts in one eye and refused to be operated upon, saying he didn't need more than one eye. Then his other eye had become affected and the subsequent surgery was unsuccessful.

His father was seventy years old. Konrad knew he had home help. When he visited he always brought a couple of daily newspapers along; his father liked Konrad to read aloud the op-eds and letters to the editor concerning current events. But first he had to read out the stock market listings for two equity funds in which his father had an unspecified number of shares.

Konrad was unable to interpret his father's reactions, after all, his eyes gave nothing away. And he did not ask. He had once and his father, after a sudden, impatient toss of the head, had replied: Unchanged.

Sometimes his father asked Konrad how things were with him, and if he did have something to relate, his father seemed to listen patiently but did not come with any follow-up questions and usually an oppressive silence would then arise, prior to his father puncturing it with a laconic *well*. This particular evening his father was more taciturn and preoccupied than usual, and when Konrad opened the pages of one of the newspapers, he had said: No, no, not today.

Is anything wrong? Konrad asked.

No, he said.

After that they sat in silence for quite a while, before his father said: You're not exactly talkative.

I probably take after you, Konrad brought himself to say.

Maybe, he replied, although your mother didn't say a whole lot either.

Mom, yes she did, Konrad said, she talked all the time.

No, he replied, your memory fails you.

They continued to sit in silence.

When Konrad felt he had been there long enough, he asked his father if he was tired. His father did not answer, but asked instead: Are you leaving?

I was just wondering if you were tired, Konrad said.

Tired? his father said, and after a few moments added: Before you go, please fetch me a bottle of wine and a glass.

Konrad stood up.

I didn't say I was leaving, he said.

There were four bottles of red wine at the bottom of the cabinet; Konrad took one, went to the kitchen, opened it and brought it and a large red wine glass in to his father. He poured his father a glass, handed it to him, and then placed the bottle on the small table beside his chair.

His father groped with his free hand to ascertain where exactly the bottle was.

Thanks, he said.

Konrad hesitated; a mildness had came over his father that put him at a loss; he suddenly found it more difficult to leave than to stay. He said: Is there anything else I can do for you?

No, thank you, his father said, everything's fine now. Just fine.

Konrad was standing right beside him and his father turned his head and looked at him. That was the impression Konrad had, that his father was looking at him, and he thought: I haven't done anything to him.

And while Konrad stood allowing his father to look at him, his father let go of the glass. Again, Konrad had the distinct impression that was the case – his father had let go of the glass, it had not slipped from his grasp. The glass landed on his father's lap, as did most of the wine. Konrad picked up the glass and placed it on the table. His father got to his feet but remained standing still.

Just a moment, Konrad said.

He hurried to the kitchen, grabbed a tea towel and roll of kitchen paper. His father was standing in the same spot, his mouth half-open. Konrad blotted up the wine from the sunken area of the leather seat.

You can sit back down now, he said.

His father sat. Konrad pressed the tea towel against his wet trouser thighs and thought: I haven't been this close to him since I was a child. He felt how hard and thin the thighs had become.

Okay, it's fine now, his father said.

Konrad tore a long ream off the roll and dried up the wine stain from the floor. He heard his father pouring himself a new glass.

His father said: Everything was bright all of a sudden.

Bright? Konrad asked.

Yes, his father said, for a moment everything went completely bright.

Konrad went to the kitchen, threw the paper in the bin, then washed his hands. He took his time; he felt perplexed.

When he returned to the living room his father was sitting with the glass in his hand. Konrad asked if he should stay a little longer.

No, no, his father said, I'm fine now. And thanks for cleaning up for me.

It's the least I can do, Konrad said.

Yeah, maybe, his father said, but thanks all the same.

Konrad turned off all the lights, said goodbye and left.

On the street, Konrad found the next bus was not due for a quarter of an hour, so he began to walk toward downtown. He passed two stops but halted at the third. It had a shelter and a bench. He sat down.

A woman, not wearing any coat, emerged from a covered entryway about ten or fifteen meters further along the street; she walked to the edge of the pavement and stood there, her back to the road. Shortly afterwards a man came out from the same entryway, he was also inadequately dressed. He walked slowly toward her. They stood face-to-face for a few moments, not saying anything. Suddenly the man slapped her, Konrad both saw and heard it. The woman's head was thrown to the side but she did not make a sound. The man struck her again, then once more. The woman stood with her arms by her side and let it happen.

Then she took a step forward and kissed him; the man grasped her hair with one hand and steered her in front of him into the entryway. At that moment the bus came.

The scene Konrad witnessed gave rise to a sexual reaction in him, and on the bus home a short story by Anaïs Nin came to mind, in which, as he recalled, she describes a scene where a woman, standing watching a public execution, is groped by a man behind her in the packed crowd. With her making no attempt to resist, the stranger eventually penetrates her, and as the axe falls, decapitating the condemned man, she reaches orgasm.

Upon arriving home, Konrad telephoned Vibeke, but she did not answer. To compensate, he took Nin's book from the bookshelf and read the short story. It struck him while reading, but even more so afterwards, how wide off the mark he had been in his recollection.

A couple of nights later he had a dream. He had never made any attempt at interpreting dreams, he knew it was not possible, but he did not deny that they could make an impression. He dreamt about his father. There was no plot in the dream, just a face, a severe-looking, contorted face. It bore no resemblance to his father's, but he knew that it was his. It appeared and disappeared over and over. He was awoken by it pressing against his eyes, wanting to get into him.

He got up, it was half three in the morning. He drank a glass of water then went into the living room and wrote down the dream in the form of main points: "Father, not father. A face. Wanted to get inside me."

That same morning he went out to take some photographs. He took four separate photographs of the trunks of two pine trees, with a beach, the sea, horizon, and sky as a backdrop. A linear motif, composed of approximately seventy percent clouds. The dream was on his mind the entire time. It felt as though he did not want to forget it. He continued walking, past the trees, down toward the shoreline, into the motif, so to speak. Then he turned and walked to the café where he had arranged to meet Vibeke.

Vibeke put down *Journey to the End of the Night* and lit a cigarette. He sat down.

Well? she said.

Yes, he said.

The sea? she said.

Yes, he said, that too, but mostly sky and beach.

Marion

IT WAS NOT yet noon, and hot. I was lying in the shadow of one of the large birch trees at one end of the park, watching how the clouds dissolved right above me. I'd never seen it so clearly before. They came from the north and, here by the coast, went no farther.

The red-haired man passed by again, and this time I pretended not to notice him; I don't know why but he didn't interest me, I'm certain of that. There was nothing striking or interesting about him other than maybe – and only maybe, because strictly speaking even that was neither striking nor interesting – his passing by for a third time.

If he walks past one more time, I thought.

The grass I was lying on continued on the other side of the path, ending at a low hedge some twenty meters further on. Some swallows circled above me; for some reason or other I figured there must be a church nearby. I turned on my side and closed my eyes; I don't think I fell asleep although it's possible. I could hear the sound of pruning shears or some such tool.

The first thing I saw when I awoke, if I actually had slept, was him, the red-haired man, walking by a fourth time. It occurred to me he was going in the same direction as on the previous occasion. It didn't necessarily mean anything, he may have walked back the other way while I was asleep, if indeed I had been. It was no less striking for that.

I pretended not to see him. When he was out of sight I got to my feet, shook my blanket and put it in the beach basket. I wasn't running away, he hadn't scared me.

On entering the square I saw him for a fifth time. He was standing in the strip of shadow provided by a camera shop chatting to a couple, a man and woman. He didn't see me. The woman was doing the talking; she was around my age.

I sat down at an empty table under a large awning on the opposite side of the open, rectangular plaza and ordered a coffee. Suddenly he wasn't standing there anymore.

I walked directly back to the guesthouse, it wasn't far. Marion was sitting writing a letter. My name's also Marion. The room faced a garden of sorts enclosed by a high wooden fence. By garden of sorts I mean there were traces of flowerbeds but no flowers. We went down to the dining room.

While we were waiting to be served I said I had to use the gents'. I went up to the room to see if Marion had written anything about me. She'd put down only that I was out. The letter was to her mother. *We've been here four days now*, it said, and on the way back down I wondered why she had written what she did, because it wasn't true, we'd arrived in town only two days ago.

The soup had arrived; Marion was sitting eating. An aerial photograph of the city hung on the wall behind her. Yet another hung between the two windows facing the street. In the center of the photograph above Marion's head lay the park, and just behind that, looking inland from the sea, there was, sure enough, a church.

Marion didn't say much and I don't remember what we talked about. It was so hot. But afterwards, back in the room, when we were taking an afternoon nap, she asked if I'd noticed the blond waitress with the high cheekbones. I knew the one she meant.

Does she brush against you when she's serving you? she asked.

No, I said, I don't think so.

Maybe I'm just imagining it, Marion said.

She didn't say anything after that. I asked her what she meant.

Well, just that she keeps brushing against me.

She lay on her back looking up at the ceiling before closing her eyes. When I awoke – it couldn't have been much later – she was standing looking at me in the mirror.

We went out to get a coffee and sat down under the awning in the square.

Look, Marion said.

I followed the direction of her gaze but didn't understand what she meant.

I'm sure that was your brother, she said.

Where?

On the corner, together with another guy.

That's impossible, I said.

Yeah, it would be an odd coincidence, I must have been mistaken. I was so sure but I was probably wrong, some people do look alike after all, and I hardly know him.

There aren't many people who look like Peter, I said, laughing.

No, perhaps not, she said.

We sat looking at the people walking past and many of them looked at us. It was getting close to six o'clock and although no longer quite so hot it was still very warm. I ordered a beer, even though it was a little early. Marion just sat looking.

There! she said, but just at that moment I was busy watching them retract the four-meter-long awning and by the time I looked in the direction she was staring it was too late.

The guy I thought was him, your brother, Marion said.

Where? I said.

Over there, he went into that alleyway.

I got to my feet and cut diagonally across the square. I reached the alleyway, it was only a couple of meters wide but it was long. I walked to the end, or rather where another alleyway intersected it. Then I walked back.

Marion had been joined by a man who was leaning on the tabletop with both hands, resting his weight. I could see that he was talking. I couldn't face sitting down together with them, she'd just have to handle him without my help. I stood by the entrance to the restaurant watching her and waiting for her to send him packing. But she didn't; the man sat down.

Jesus, I thought.

I left and wandered the narrow streets with my bag over one shoulder and the camera over the other. I stopped at one of the stalls and bought a small bottle of rosemary oil. Then I took a right, toward the harbor.

I thought it was strange that Marion had written four days to her mother. True, we had used two days more than necessary along the way, necessary with regard to time, I mean. Because of Ochsenfurt. It hadn't been my fault, but then again it was a nice little town. Marion got drunk in *Zur blauen Traube* and disappeared with a plumber; she didn't show up again until around eleven on Sunday morning; she didn't say much but insisted on sleeping. I took a long walk along the Main. I was struck by how unremarkable famous rivers can be. Marion didn't wake up until evening. She was uncommunicative and standoffish.

Not a good night? I said.

Don't ask, she said.

I understood. She's different from me but also quite similar. I guess that's how it is: most people are different but quite similar all the same. Or maybe not.

We continued on the next day, in the late morning. It was raining.

The Cost of Friendship

HAVING DECLINED TWICE previously, I'd said yes. We'd been close at one time, years back, and had never fallen out, time and distance had merely done away with the reasons to keep in touch.

Now, out of an irrational feeling of guilt, I'd reluctantly said yes.

He was sitting just inside the entrance. He got to his feet. He was easily recognizable, although different. We exchanged a few pleasantries, then sat down.

The waitress came over, she was striking. We each ordered an aperitif. He had grown a pencil moustache. We continued to make small talk. The waitress brought our drinks. We raised our glasses.

Then he offered me a cigarette. I told him I'd given up. He asked if I minded him smoking.

Not in the slightest, I said.

He said he ought to quit as well.

Why? I asked.

You have a point there, he said, why indeed. He lit up the cigarette. He asked why I'd given up.

A heart condition, I said, and as though prompted by my answer he asked if I was still married to Nora.

Yes, I said, she's managed to put up with me.

He said he was sure that hadn't been too difficult for her, which I pretty much agreed with so I made no reply.

During the subsequent lull in conversation he reached for the menu. I did the same. The waitress came and we ordered.

I figured that since he'd wanted to meet me, there must be something he wanted to talk about, so I said: Well?

Well, he said. Then, after a brief pause: Cheers.

I drained my glass. I said I had to go to the restroom.

There was nobody else there so I put two tens into the condom machine – a tendency I have. I took my time and when I returned a bottle had arrived on the table and there was red wine in the glasses.

I told him I couldn't remember when we'd last met or what the occasion was.

He said it'd been at my place about twelve or thirteen years ago.

Go on, I said.

It was just before you moved, he said, you and Nora were having a going-away party.

Really? I said.

Don't you remember? he asked.

Tell me more, I said.

You even made a speech.

Oh Jesus, I said.

It was a nice speech, he said, you spoke about friendship.

I didn't reply; I didn't feel completely at ease. Fortunately the wait-ress arrived with the food. She really was stunning, and when she left our table I commented upon it, in the hope of changing the subject.

Oh? he said, and began to eat.

Have you given up looking at beautiful women? I asked.

Good heavens, no, he said, at least I don't think so, but you can't look at all of them.

You've given up so, I said.

He took a bite of food and did not reply.

We ate in silence for a while. I wanted to ask how his wife was but I couldn't remember her name so I didn't; some people tend to interpret my bad memory as a lack of interest, which they might be right about to an extent.

Instead, in order to say something, I asked if he was still in touch with the old crowd.

Some of them, he said.

Henrik? I asked.

No, he said, his reply sufficiently brusque to rouse my curiosity.

No? I asked.

No, he said, and continued eating.

I made up my mind not to be the first one to speak again. I ate and drank wine. The waitress came and filled up our glasses. He didn't even look up, just went on eating, determinedly, I thought, perhaps on account of his chewing being accompanied now and again by a snap of his jaws.

Eventually, he said: He came between Eva and me. But maybe you knew that, seeing as he was the one you asked about.

Henrik did? I said.

You didn't know about that? he said.

No, I said.

So I have nothing to do with him anymore, he said, and set about eating again.

But you and Eva are still married? I asked.

He nodded.

I was becoming annoyed at having to drag the words out of him; I wasn't the one who'd asked to meet up. I put down my knife and fork and looked around. I couldn't see the waitress. I drank some wine. I glanced at him now and again but he didn't so much as peek up at me.

I poured myself more wine, then I said: Would you prefer if I left?

He looked up, in puzzlement, as though suddenly awoken.

What? he said.

Your own company seems to be more than enough for you, I said.

He stared at me; it was quite uncomfortable.

So just leave then, he said, at long last, I didn't think it was necessary to talk the entire time.

He picked up his cigarette packet and plucked out a cigarette that he tapped three times on the tablecloth before lighting; it was a ritualistic action, and in a way suited the thin moustache he was sporting.

I'm sorry, he said.

Me too, I said.

We raised our glasses.

The waitress came and poured the remainder of the bottle into our glasses. I looked at her and asked for another bottle. She didn't make eye contact.

When she'd gone, he said that it'd been such a long time since we last met that while waiting for me he'd wondered if it had been *too* long, and whether we'd recognize one another, that possibly how we each saw ourselves had altered, after all, it was only reasonable to expect we'd changed, at least in relation to one another, since our interaction had ceased.

They were the words I had used in my speech that night, he said, I had said that what threatened a friendship was the cessation of interaction.

Did I say that? I said.

Yes, he said.

And you remember it? I said.

Why wouldn't I? he said.

The Toilet Bag

ANYTHING ELSE you'd like? she asked.

No, thank you.

She was standing in front of him, her body language more pronounced than before. And when she finally turned and left, she took her words with her across the floor.

Once again he felt hot inside and thought: if I wasn't me or if I were that part of me that represents what is forbidden, I wouldn't have let her go.

He had come here several times previously to write. But this time the words would not fall in place. He did not know why. It made him restless.

He went out. It had grown warmer. Some tables and chairs had been placed on the pavement outside a pastry shop in the center of town; he sat down.

I shouldn't have let her go, he thought.

Then he thought, I shouldn't have left, I should have gone down to the reception or the dining room and asked for another beer – then she would have understood.

He finished his coffee and went back to the guesthouse. There was a man standing in front of the reception desk.

Isn't there anybody here? the man asked.

Have you rung the bell?

Lots of times.

They often take a while.

Are you staying here?

Yes. I'll go see if I can find somebody.

He walked through the dining room and into the kitchen. The sink was full of cups and saucers and he was slightly taken aback because the waitress had said he was the only guest.

Apart from the one leading to the dining room, there were two other doors. He knocked on one. No one answered. He turned the handle. The door was locked. The other one led to a passage ending in a small, enclosed yard. He returned to the kitchen. The landlady was standing in the doorway of the room that had been locked.

What can I do for you? she said in an unfriendly tone.

He explained.

We're full up, she said. You can tell him all the rooms are occupied.

You want *me* to tell him?

Why not? After all, you are asking on his behalf. Besides, I'm not dressed.

This last part was clearly untrue, still it was the first part of her answer that confused him the most.

He made no reply.

He went back to the reception. There was nobody there. He thought it unreasonable for the man to leave – he had been gone no more than a couple of minutes – so he stood in the visibly empty room and called out:

Is there anybody here!

It sounded much louder than he had intended, angry almost, so to avoid a possible reply he hurried out of the guesthouse and around the nearest street corner. Then he stopped for a moment, before continuing with short, angry steps.

I'm leaving, he thought, I'm not staying another day in that damn guesthouse.

He had taken the street he was accustomed to walking and upon coming to the Balzac he went inside. It was still early and the premises were almost empty. The publican gave him a nod; one of recognition he presumed, and he immediately found himself in a more conciliatory mood, both in regard to the guesthouse and to himself.

He might not know who I am, he thought, but he recognizes me.

He sat upright at his table and drank two beers. He thought about why he had left the guesthouse earlier that day and his reason for returning. He could picture the waitress clearly, her upright posture, chest almost thrust forward. And the contour of her back as she bent over. No, that wasn't her, that was the chambermaid.

So what, he thought boldly. One of them. Or both. I've had far too few women. For a while he indulged in titillating imaginings where the two women, first one, then the other, played the lead. He was completely aware of how removed these images were from any world of reality where he himself could play a supporting role, nevertheless he enjoyed them, slightly guiltily, but defiantly. And when there was no more to be had from the images he paid and returned to the guesthouse.

There was no one at the reception but when he made it up the stairs to the narrow hallway he saw the chambermaid coming out of the room opposite his and locking the door behind her. She glanced at him and gave a barely perceptible nod. He recalled the waitress had said she was under the weather; he was just about to ask how she was but hesitated and by then it was too late; he couldn't very well shout it out after her. He watched her disappear down the stairs, and then remembered he had meant to ask for a beer, so he followed her. She must have heard his footsteps because she stopped.

Would it be possible to get a beer?

A beer?

Yes.

Just a moment.

He stood waiting. It took a while. And when she did eventually come back she had neither a glass nor a bottle opener with her. He settled at asking for a bottle opener. That took a while too. Not much around here goes according to plan, he thought impatiently, but when she showed up again he was immediately placated by the apologetic look on her face.

I'm sorry, she said, but Mrs. Langer. . .

He presumed that was the landlady. He nodded and gave her a knowing smile, he thought he could take that liberty.

Clearly she did not; she shot him a severe look and said: We each have our cross to bear.

Offended by her rebuke and hurt that the consideration he had shown had not gone down well, he asked, somewhat brusquely, for a glass.

I thought you had a glass, she said and went to fetch one.

Actually, yes, maybe I do, he called after her, don't bother!

He went up to his room. He opened the bottle and put it to his lips. I don't need a fucking glass, he said to himself.

He flopped down on the bed but no sooner had he done so than there was a knock at the door. While he was contemplating whether or not to answer the door opened and the chambermaid came in holding a glass. He jumped up, conscience-stricken because he had been lying on the bedspread with his shoes on.

The chambermaid placed the new glass beside the old one. It looked silly and he said: I thought perhaps it had been tidied away.

Doesn't matter.

What a way to answer, he thought, and something dismissive in the manner she said it annoyed him. Rather rashly, he said:

I thought you were sick.

Oh?

I must have misunderstood.

She took the old glass and left. He looked around for the empty beer bottle from that afternoon but could not find it. He checked the toilet, but it wasn't there either. So someone *had* been in his room since he left. That in itself was not so strange; whoever it was might have thought he may need the glass later.

He was on the point of settling for that explanation when he noticed his toilet bag was not in its usual spot on the shelf above the sink but lay unzipped on the windowsill. He knew for certain he never left it open; that was on account of his shyness with the fact it contained a packet of condoms.

There was nothing missing from the toilet bag but the thought of someone having opened it and looked inside filled him with dread. He felt laid bare, yes, he felt as if whoever had seen the packet of condoms had at the same time – and by virtue of it – read his innermost thoughts, had seen his hidden self.

He removed his shoes and lay under the duvet with his clothes on, before getting out of bed and locking the door, then lying down again. But he soon realized he was not going to be able to sleep and that lying there doing nothing only made matters worse, only compounded the growing feeling of being forsaken, forlorn. Even so, he did not get up but thought: it's how it is, this is the essence of my life, after all, the rest is just work, recreation, an escape from acknowledgment.

He'd been lying like that for a while, digging himself deeper down, when he heard a man outside the door say in a loud, clear voice:

And bring an extra glass if you'd like to share it with me.

He heard no reply, he did not hear anything more at all. He threw off the duvet and walked to the door. He tried looking through the keyhole. He could not see anything either.

Nothing for Nothing

INGRID GOT that faraway look in her eyes that he did not like because it meant he had drifted to the periphery. He had been enjoying himself, but now he was not enjoying himself any longer.

He looked over at the table where the German couple were sitting. He thought: he's much older than her. She's not much older than me. She's a good-looking woman.

He turned to Ingrid, but she was preoccupied with the circle dance in front of the bar. Most of the participants were Greek, the few tourists who had ventured onto the floor were either drunk or halfway there, and nearly all were women.

"They're pretending it's impromptu," he said, because he had heard at the hotel that it was not.

"Relax," Ingrid said.

"I'm trying to."

"Don't be so negative," she said. "You can see that people are having a good time."

"Right."

"There's nothing wrong with people having a good time."

"They don't realize it's all rehearsed."

Ingrid shrugged and made no reply.

The German lady suddenly looked over at him and smiled. It was a friendly, pleasant smile and he responded in kind.

"Do you know her?" Ingrid asked.

"Who?"

"The woman you smiled at."

"No. They're staying at the hotel."

"Why did you say *who*?"

"Because I didn't know who you meant."

"Oh, for God's sake."

He did not reply.

"I want an ouzo now," Ingrid said.

"Not again tonight, surely. You know how that turned out the other day."

"That was because I'd eaten shellfish."

She waved the waiter over and ordered.

The atmosphere in the bar grew livelier.

The German lady looked at him again. She was not smiling. He could see Ingrid was busy watching the dancing. He raised his glass, the German lady did the same. She still did not smile. He looked away.

Then he sat there in thought. After a while it occurred to him:

nobody knows what I'm thinking. Imagine if Ingrid knew what I was thinking right now.

Ingrid said: "I want to dance."

He just nodded; his thoughts were elsewhere.

She cut in between two Greek men. Yes, he thought, of course.

He looked over at the German lady. Then looked at her husband and again thought: He's older than her. And I'm younger than her. And she's looking at me. He thought: I'm looking at her now, and if Ingrid sees me doing it, then that's fine, it wouldn't do her any harm to have something to think about. He stared at her, waiting for her to return his gaze, and when she did, he raised his glass, thinking: Ingrid's welcome to see. The German lady also raised her glass; she did not smile. She's probably about five years older than me, he thought. Then he looked over at Ingrid, saw her smiling to the Greek on her left; he was young and good-looking. Yes, of course, he thought. The German lady looked at him, without smiling, but for a long time. He held her gaze and did not smile either. If Ingrid can do it, he thought, then so can I. He looked at Ingrid, she was looking at the Greek and smiling. Then he looked at the German man. He's at least ten years older than her, he thought, she can't be too happy about that, nor can he, apart from his taking pride in having a pretty wife ten years his junior, but I'd imagine it causes problems.

Ingrid was dancing and smiling at the young, good-looking Greek.

He's at least five years younger than her, he thought, and she's always said she only likes men who are at least the same age as her. Then he thought: but I've always said I could never be interested in an older woman.

He took a drink, then went to the men's room; he had to go through two doors before he found it. When he came out he met the German lady. He stopped, and she did too. They kissed, without exchanging a word. Then she pulled away and continued on. He put one hand in his trouser pocket and went back to the table. Ingrid was looking at the young Greek, then said something and laughed. She's flirting, he thought.

Then she came and sat down. She was smiling, warm and happy.

"I see you're having a good time," he said.

"Yes, it was nice."

"Well, it's not the end of the world," he said.

She looked at him.

"No, that would be silly," she said.

"It would," he said, "wouldn't it."

She looked at him.

"But you never know," she said.

The German lady returned from the toilet, she looked at him.

That's a sure thing, he thought.

Ingrid gestured to the waiter and ordered an ouzo.

"Hope you know what you're doing."

She did not reply.

He glanced at the German lady and made eye contact.

He poured white wine into his glass.

The waiter brought over the ouzo.

Now it's her turn to go to the toilets first, he thought.

"Won't you come up and dance?" Ingrid asked.

"And ruin all your fun?" he said.

"For God's sake. Will we just leave then?"

"No, why? I'm perfectly fine."

"All right then. Cheers."

She kissed me, he thought. He looked over at her, she was saying something to her husband; he then said something to her and smiled. She's pulling the wool over his eyes, he thought.

"I'll just dance on my own," Ingrid said.

"On your own?"

She stood up and slipped between two Greeks, not the same ones as last time, one of them was her age, the other older. He watched her for a while, without seeing anything that could justify his own thoughts, then looked at the German lady until she met his gaze. She nodded to him in a way he didn't understand. Then she stood up and approached him.

"*Gehen wir mal spazieren?*" she said.

He didn't understand.

"You speak English?"

"Yes?"

"You take me with you for a walk?"

"Yes – no – my wife . . ."

"You are not free?"

"No, my wife . . ."

"I see. Why did you kiss me then?"

"I . . ." He felt himself blush, could not think what to say.

"I see," she said, then left.

He took a sip of his drink. He did not know where to look. He took another sip. He looked down at the stained, white tablecloth. Then he lit up a cigarette, and sat looking at the people dancing, without seeing them. If she doesn't come soon I'm leaving, he thought. He drained the glass and refilled it. If she doesn't come by the time I've finished this then I'm leaving.

Then she came.

"What did she want?" she asked.

"I couldn't understand what she said."

She looked at him, he did not return her gaze but he was aware of it. She did not say any more.

"I wouldn't mind leaving now," he said.

"Oh?"

"Assuming it's possible for you to tear yourself away from all your admirers."

"Oh, for God's sake."

"Of course there's nothing stopping me from leaving on my own."

"No, of course not."

"You probably won't have any problem getting someone to walk you home."

"No. And anyway I'm capable of getting home by myself."

"Right, well I'll be off then."

"Have you paid?"

He took out his wallet and signaled to the waiter.

"Have I done something to upset you?" she said.

He did not answer.

"Have I done something to upset you?" she repeated.

"You? No. What could you have done? You're just dancing and having a good time, you haven't done anything to upset me."

"There's nothing wrong with me dancing, is there?"

"Dancing and having a good time. No, of course not, that's what I'm saying."

The waiter came. He paid. The waiter left.

"So you don't mind me staying a little longer?" she said.

"Would it matter?"

"I'm not sure."

"No, I gathered that."

She did not say anything. He stood up.

"You have the money," she said.

"How much do you need?"

"I want to have another ouzo."

He took out his wallet and put a hundred on the table. Then he turned and left. He walked out into warm, almost sultry darkness and thought: she didn't come with me.

It was not far to walk. When he was halfway up the steps to the hotel, he stopped. He thought: I'm coming back alone, before Ingrid. The night porter will think she's found someone else. I'll spare him the amusement.

He looked around. The steps continued up past the hotel entrance and disappeared in the darkness. That was where he went. From where he was standing he could clearly see the lit-up entrance to the hotel. His thoughts alternated between Ingrid and the German lady. I should have gone with her, he thought, so Ingrid could feel what it's like.

He sat down, lit a cigarette and waited, after that he lit another. He could picture the German lady more and more clearly. Fuck being faithful, he thought, this is the thanks you get. Being faithful is for nothing.

Then she came – together with the German couple. They were chatting and laughing. Suddenly he was convinced they must be able to see him and he shrank back. The German man held the door open for them, and they disappeared into the hotel.

He remained sitting, because they might be standing talking before going their separate ways. Besides it only served her right if she began to wonder where he went.

He lit a cigarette, and thought: I won't say anything. She can say what she wants, I won't reply.

He got to his feet, walked down the steps and into the hotel. He nodded to the night porter, could afford to now, having come in last.

She was pretending to be asleep but had left his bedside lamp on. She doesn't know that I know when she got in, he thought. She doesn't know that I know she's not sleeping, and I can't tell her that I know. She's pretending to sleep because she doesn't want it to be obvious she just got in, wants to make out she's better than that.

He undressed, switched off the light, and pulled the sheet over him. He lay for a while thinking about Ingrid pretending to sleep, and about the German lady. He could picture her very clearly.

Next morning he got up before her, as usual. He did not wake her. He dressed and went out.

It was hot, but there was a very light breeze coming off the ocean; it was so early that the low-lying island beyond the entrance to the harbor had not yet dissolved in the heat haze.

He walked along the quayside. The red, green, and white fishing boats had returned to port long ago, and they lay in the shelter of the breakwater with yellow nylon nets coiled up behind the motor housing.

He crossed the narrow canal linking the harbor to the lake. There were three outdoor cafés side by side along the west bank of the lake. He found a table and ordered a cappuccino and some toast with ham.

He wondered if Ingrid would come, she knew where to look for him after all.

When he had finished eating, he went over to the kiosk and bought a postcard with a picture of the lake on it. He returned to the table. He ordered a bottle of beer. Then he wrote on the postcard to his mother. He wrote: *Dear Mother. Right now I'm sitting where I have put an X on the picture. They say that the lake (that's it in the picture) is very deep. In the old days they thought it was bottomless. I'm very well. Everything here is quite cheap, but I don't think I care particularly for the Greeks. They seem rather primitive. Tell you more when I see you. Ingrid says to say hello. Yours, Bjørn*

He turned the card over and put an X on it. Then he read through what he had written and was satisfied. It's all about saying something using very few words, he thought.

He was almost finished his beer when Ingrid arrived.

"Hi. Have a good sleep?"

"Lovely."

She ordered an omelette and tea. She looked at the teenagers diving from the side of the quay and said:

"I don't know how they have the nerve."

"What?"

"I'd never dare swim in a place where it was so far to the bottom."

"Same thing, isn't it, as long as you can swim."

"It's not the same."

"Just as easy to drown in two meters of water as in a hundred."

"You don't understand what I mean."

He kept his annoyance in check and didn't respond, then thought: so typical of a woman. But, after all, that's what I like about her so much, that she's so feminine, so helpless.

He put his hand on hers, and with a smile – the smile she had often told him she loved – said:

"I understand more than you think."

She gave him a wary, quizzical look.

He said:

"Not for nothing that I love you so much, is it?"

The Wake

THERE WERE MANY who laid wreaths. Everyone said she'd been a good person who was valued highly. I didn't cry. Georg was the last to lay a wreath. He said it hurt that she was dead. He said he couldn't understand why she was no longer alive, when there was someone who needed her. I didn't cry then either, because I'd done all my crying beforehand. After that they sang a hymn and the coffin was carried out. It was covered with fresh flowers. When the coffin was lowered, Georg placed a hand on my shoulder. He probably meant well, but he shouldn't have done it, because it only made things worse. "Earth to earth, ashes to ashes, dust to dust. In sure and certain hope of the resurrection to eternal life." Then, when it was over, the priest came and shook my hand. He said to always remember that God had a purpose with everything, and I turned away. Many of the others came over to shake my hand, and I asked Georg if we couldn't try to get away from them all. When we got outside the walls of the graveyard, it began to rain. Georg clapped me on the shoulder.

"Let's go to the Cellar and get a cup of coffee," he said.

We walked down a flight of stairs; there were lots of people and the smoke was thick under the ceiling. We found an unoccupied table, and I could see the legs of the people passing on the pavement outside from slightly above the knees and down. Georg waved to a waiter and I ordered a double brandy with soda. Georg looked at me. The waiter didn't move. "Same for me," Georg said.

"You shouldn't force yourself to forget," he said.

"I wasn't planning on forgetting."

The waiter brought the glasses and the soda. Neither of us said anything for a while. We just raised our glasses, nodded to one another, and drank. Georg offered me a cigarette.

"There's no point in not talking about it," I said.

"A lot of the time it helps to talk," Georg said.

"Making out you're stronger than you are is just plain stupid."

"You're handling it very well."

"I just feel so damned sorry for her."

"There's no need to. It's all over now."

"We were supposed to go to Paris in the summer. She was so looking forward to it. In the final few days she didn't talk about anything else."

Georg made no reply and I sipped my drink. He drummed on the tabletop with his fingers. I drained my glass and signaled to the waiter. I asked for another brandy and loud music suddenly started coming from the loudspeaker high up under the ceiling. The music was turned down, and I said that we were supposed to go to Paris twice previously but nothing came of it. Georg said there was no point crying over spilt milk, and I said I agreed, but he was forgetting that she was dead. We drank, and I sat watching the legs outside the window.

"You have a lot of good memories," Georg said.

"Yes. However, I'd be happy not to have them. They're not good any longer. They're not good now she's dead."

"I understand."

"It's the memories that keep me awake every single night and bring me to tears."

"It'll pass."

"Yeah, you'd know all about it."

"I've never lost anyone close to me but it can only be natural for it to pass."

"Sounds like you really know what you're talking about."

He didn't reply, and I immediately said that he mustn't take me too seriously. "That's all right," he said. We raised our glasses and drank. The spirits began to have an effect.

"That damned priest said there was a purpose to everything."

"I heard him."

"I don't believe that at all."

"Me neither."

"I don't believe there's a purpose to anything."

"Exactly. That was what I was trying to say when I laid the wreath."

"It was nice, what you said."

"You think?"

"There was no one who expressed how irreplaceable she was as well as you did."

"I'm glad you think so. I tried to say it as clearly as possible."

"That's what makes for a good speech, saying what you ought to say and no more. And you managed that. Cheers."

I had to excuse myself for a moment. From the restroom I could hear the rain. I washed my hands and went back into the restaurant. Georg had been joined by a girl. Her name was Astrid. I recognized her. She offered her condolences, and I said, "Welcome to the wake." She didn't know whether or not to smile and looked a little foolish. Georg said that if Lilly were here we could've had a really nice time. "Don't let that stop you," I said. Astrid blushed slightly and Georg said that wasn't what he meant.

"You shouldn't mourn if it doesn't come naturally," I said.

"Apart from you, there were few people who held Lilly as dear as I did."

The waiter came over with two glasses and a bottle of soda. I asked for another brandy. Astrid and Georg raised their glasses. The waiter brought my brandy and I raised mine. Georg smiled at me. "Pay no attention to what I'm saying," I said. Georg screwed up his eyes and smiled. "I'm not myself," I said. "I've never been bereaved before." "Cheers," Astrid said. "Cheers," the two of us replied.

"I valued Lilly as highly as anyone I've known," Georg said.

"She was too good for this world," I said.

"No one's too good for this world. It's exactly people like Lilly that we need."

"She was good through and through," I said, "there wasn't an ounce of badness in her."

"She must have been wonderful," Astrid said.

"No need to be sarcastic."

"I didn't mean to be."

"You're being sarcastic because you didn't know her. She didn't have a bad bone in her body, did she Georg?"

"Well, I certainly valued her as highly as anyone I've known."

We continued drinking. Georg offered cigarettes around. Astrid sat watching me. I was slightly drunk. I raised my glass with both of them.

"It's good to drink," Georg said.

"Damn right," I said, "I'll get the next round."

We finished our drinks. "Waiter!" I shouted, and all the customers at the tables around us turned and looked at me.

"Shush!" Georg said.

"Waiter!" I called out again.

The waiter came over and said that if I didn't stop shouting I'd have to leave. I piped down and told him we'd like to order. "You'll just have to wait your turn," he said, and left. Astrid looked at me and smiled. I smiled back.

"Let's have a nice time," I said. "Let's forget why we're sitting here."

"The trick is to accept reality," Georg said.

"Yes," said Astrid.

"You're right," I said.

"The trick is to live in the moment."

"Yes. I don't give a shit about Paris."

"What do you mean?"

"I was supposed to be in Paris this summer. Together with Lilly. It's not going to happen now she's dead, and I don't give a shit."

"That makes sense."

"The only thing that makes sense is not to give a shit about anything."

"Yes. You should just take pleasure in what is. Not what has been and what hasn't."

"Well put," I said. The waiter came to our table and asked what we'd like. "I didn't mean to make a racket," I said. "Fine, you just can't be yelling like that," he said. "Three brandies and a soda," I said. He left.

"I'll tell you one thing," I said, "while I still had Lilly I often thought how nice it would be to be free."

"Everyone feels that way," Georg said.

"It's a horrible way to feel," I said, "I'm never going to marry again."

"You can't say that for certain."

"I damn well can. Being married is a mixed blessing. It's like a job that you like. Most of the time it's fine but if something's not right then you're held accountable. You shouldn't have to be held accountable. That's the worst thing about being married. I'm telling you both, as a friend, don't get married if you can avoid it. No harm to Lilly but she could always tell by looking at me when something wasn't quite right. When a man gives himself to several women it's not so dangerous, but when he gives himself to just one, then he's done for. I know what I'm talking about."

After saying this I felt like having more to drink. I couldn't see the waiter anywhere. "Where the hell has the waiter got to," I said. "He'll show up," Astrid said. I couldn't see him anyplace. "Waiter!" I shouted. The couple at the neighboring table began to laugh. "Waiter!" I yelled as loudly as I could. "Now we're going to get thrown out," Georg said. The waiter came. His face was red. "If you'd be so kind as to remove yourself from the premises," he said, grabbing hold of me by the lapel. "Don't touch me," I said. "I'll leave, but don't touch me." Everyone in the restaurant was looking at us. Some people were laughing. I took a few banknotes from my pocket and handed them to Georg. He smiled. Astrid was looking in another direction. I left. Outside it was still raining.

An Uplifting Funeral

THE DAY BEGAN so well, I'd had a good night's sleep. This is going to be one of the better days, Paul, I told myself. And when I arrived at the small park where, if the weather is fine, I usually sit and read the newspaper, even the bench closest to the stop sign was free. I like to sit there; you see so much impatience at a stop sign, even witness the odd accident. Not that I'm crazy about accidents, but, for example, if for some reason an airplane were to explode in the sky, I wouldn't mind being one of the people – preferably the only one – who witnessed it. Yes indeed, Paul, I said to myself, don't rule out this being one of the better days.

I know some people think of me as an old grump but that's certainly not the whole truth. Whenever a bright spot appears in my life I latch right onto it and can find myself crying out within: at last, at long last! Not that this happens very often, of course, that's not how the world is. But, for instance, a little over a month ago . . . no, it was longer than that . . . never mind, it's not a good example.

Anyway, I was sitting there, with nothing weighing on my mind, when I suddenly saw my twin brother John tottering along the sidewalk.

I quickly raised the newspaper in front of my face. I fervently hoped he hadn't seen me, but then I heard his voice:

"So, Paul, pretending not to have seen me, are you?"

He's always been that way, blunt and insensitive.

I smiled politely, as though I hadn't heard what he said.

"Oh, it's you," I said. "It's been a long time."

He sat down next to me and immediately started going on about exactly how long it had been.

"Almost two years to the day before mother died, and that was nine years ago."

"Oh," I said, "has it really been that long?"

"I'd expected to see you at the funeral at least."

"Well," I said, "that's kind of you."

Despite my friendly tone he continued to lecture me about the nine-year absence, saying I could have sent a telegram or some flowers at the very least. And so on. It was stupid. So just to rile him, I admit, I asked what his mother had died from. This certainly riled him.

"You're asking me that after nine . . . *my* mother? What do you mean by *my* mother? Are you not her son anymore either?"

Although I'm rather partial to disasters, I strongly dislike being the center of attention. Because of my appearance – my face is rather piglike (due partly to an illness, I won't specify which) – I know that should I find myself in a dispute in public, then any onlookers will automatically assign all blame to me. And I was now about to land in just such a situation due to my brother's very vocal indignation. An obnoxious brat had come to a halt a few meters away, and the pedestrians on the sidewalk were slowing down or stopping altogether. I felt uneasy and got up to leave. But John wasn't having any of it; he grabbed me by the arm and pulled me back onto the bench. Oh, if only I'd been strong! I was helpless. Utterly helpless. I was in the grip of a lunatic who the spectators would undoubtedly view as the more normal of the two of us. And who on top of that, was my twin brother. You can't call the police because your twin brother is holding you by the arm. They wouldn't understand.

There was one positive, however. Owing most likely to the effort required to keep a grip on me, he had stopped yelling. And I didn't say a word for fear he would start up again.

While I sat there trying to figure out how to get away – I even considered setting fire to him, I always carry a lighter with a high flame – there occurred one of those rare coincidences that turn out to be in your favor: an accident took place. I heard the screech of brakes followed by a loud bang, and glancing over my shoulder I saw a moped on its side and a seemingly lifeless old man in front of the wheels of a taxi. My brother, who probably hasn't seen as many accidents as I have, loosened his grip on my arm momentarily, and I took advantage of the opportunity to hurry away as quickly as I could. I can safely say I haven't moved so fast in fifteen years. My legs creaked and whined, and after walking hard like this for at least a couple of minutes I couldn't go any further. If he caught up with me then so be it.

But he didn't come after me, I was in the clear. I was nearly dead from exhaustion but out of danger. I sat down heavily on some steps, where I remained like a vagrant until I thought my legs might carry me again, at least a short distance.

I found myself close to a library and, figuring I could get a proper rest within, went inside.

I sank down into a chair by the magazines and periodicals. Oh, how my weary body enjoyed the comfort! And I must have nodded off because the next thing I knew someone was shaking me, and I heard an angry voice whisper in my ear:

"No sleeping allowed here."

It was a rule I could understand – how would it look if everyone in the library were to sleep – but I didn't like the tone in which it was said. He was a young man with a dreary moustache, drooping at both corners of his mouth.

"I can't hear what you're saying," I replied, in the low voice you use in a library.

Unfortunately, he wasn't the brightest librarian, he probably hadn't read enough good novels. He stood for a moment, studying my ugly face, then pointed toward the exit.

This infuriated me, but I took a magazine from the shelf and pretended to ignore him. Maintaining my composure took quite an effort on my behalf, and when he grabbed me by the arm, the same arm my twin brother had manhandled me by a short time ago, I felt my anger grow so absolutely justified that I could no longer hold back. I stood up and said with as much voice as I could summon:

"How dare you touch me, you . . . lout!"

My words were spoken loudly, but no matter how just my cause, I knew I would not win. I exited the library tearfully, I admit. I was still crying long after I left, I felt the world was against me. But after a while I pulled myself together. There, there, Paul, I said to myself, you've been through all this before, it doesn't matter. Life will soon be over anyway, and then it won't make any difference that you were ugly, lonely, and unhappy.

One day not long afterwards I turned eighty. Whether due to this or some other reason, I suffered an acute attack of melancholy. I would go as far as to claim it was an unusually acute attack. Being unable to talk myself out of it, I went down to the corner shop and bought two bottles of beer that I drank as quickly as I could. Then I lay down, but it was too early in the morning and I couldn't sleep. Instead, for some unfathomable reason, I got it into my head to take a ride on a bus. Yes, Paul, I said to myself, why not?

I grabbed my money and went to the bus stop. I got on a bus without knowing where it was headed. I didn't want to ask because they never give you a proper answer. When the conductor came I handed him a large bill and said I wanted to go to the end of the line. He didn't look at me so everything went fine.

He gave me back a lot of change so I knew the bus wasn't going very far. Still, it stopped long before I would have thought. It wasn't a nice area. There was a large factory and a long line of identical apartment blocks. The beer wanted out so I looked around for somewhere to take a leak. There wasn't anywhere so I began to walk. I probably went in the wrong direction. It was a very long street, but there was nowhere I could relieve myself, not even an entryway. Finally I saw a shop and I walked as quickly as I could to make it in time. There was a woman behind the counter who was almost as ugly as me. That gave me hope. But after looking me over she shook her head.

"But what will I do?" I asked.

"This is a shop," she said.

"I'm aware of that," I replied.

"Don't get smart with me," she said.

I hurried out, walked a few meters back the way I'd come and took a leak against the wall of a building. It was high time. Oh, so much came out, it seemed like it would never end. And of course I was seen. There was no ignominy from which I was to be spared. I heard some people shouting angrily and a woman opened a window nearby and said:

"You ought to be ashamed of yourself, at your age!"

"Oh, if you only knew," I answered, without looking at her. Then

I walked away. I tried to walk slowly but it wasn't easy. Although I'm not sure why I bothered, it wasn't as if any of them imagined I'd any dignity.

I made my way back to where the bus had stopped but there was no bus there so I continued on. I soon came to a small open square with a fountain and lots of pigeons. I sat down on a bench and looked at the passersby. There were so many good-looking people. Especially the young women; how beautiful they can be before motherhood takes its toll.

I hadn't been sitting long when something unusual happened. An elderly woman came and sat down next to me, on the same bench. Well, I figured, she must have very poor eyesight.

My initial thought was to get up and leave before any funny stuff could arise, but it was such a rare, almost foreign feeling to sit on the same bench as a woman, so I remained seated. Perhaps someone who didn't know either of us might even think we were together, I thought. Or, at the very least, that we know each other. That's the stuff daydreams are made of.

As I sat there it occurred to me that it was my birthday, and I felt a stirring of aggression within. I quickly got to my feet and walked back to the bus stop. I was angry and unafraid, so I inquired when the bus would leave. It was to depart in a few minutes. I was angry the entire way home and when I alighted at the bus stop I went straight into the nearest restaurant and ordered a pint of beer. Nobody was going to prevent me celebrating my own eightieth birthday, let them just try. It was a good anger and it didn't let up; when I'd finished my drink I was still just as angry. I said a whole lot of aggressive things to the world at large – in my own head, of course. And when an elderly man came over to my table, I was intent on not giving up.

"You must be Hornemann," he said, and I thought bitterly: once seen, always seen. But I nodded, even though I didn't know who he was.

"I was sitting over there looking at you," he said, "and I thought to myself that can be none other than Paul Hornemann."

"Yes, one runs true to form," I said.

"But you don't recognize me, do you?" he asked enthusiastically. He must have had more to drink than me.

"No."

"Holt," he said. "Frank Holt. We taught together at the high school in A."

If my failed life had any other beginning than at conception, it was at A. I have no intention of going into this at length, not now or ever; suffice to say I should never have had any students. I discovered too late that my knowledge could not make up for my appearance. The students had great fun at my expense and things ended badly. Very badly.

Enough about that. But the unexpected meeting with my former colleague Holt – whom, by the way, I still did not remember – was therefore anything but pleasant.

"Well, that's a long time ago," I said.

"Yes, a lot of water has flowed into the sea since then," he said, and right then I knew I wasn't going to enjoy his company. If he'd been shy, then he could have been excused for coming out with that kind of twaddle, but he wasn't.

"Yes, it flows and flows," I replied, "and still the water level never gets high enough."

He looked slightly puzzled, but asked if he could sit down all the same. I hesitated, but what was the point when the final answer would be yes anyway? I never learn.

He wanted to buy me a beer, but there I drew the line, so we ordered one each. He immediately began to reminisce and I realized to my relief that he had already left A the year after I'd started. All the things he remembered! And only good things, pleasant things. He must be happy, I thought, and when the stream of recollections began to thin out I said:

"So many good memories."

"Yes, you can live a long time on them."

"Then you'll probably reach a fine old age, Holt."

He smiled confidently.

"Who knows. There's many a slip twixt cup and lip."

"True, true. You sure have a way with words."

"Every day is a gift," he said enthusiastically. I was speechless. It was like listening to my mother, and she certainly wasn't someone you wanted to emulate.

"It's just like hearing my mother," I said, "and she lived to be over ninety."

He beamed.

"You don't say," he said. "Yes, I'd love to live to see the next millennium. Just imagine it, Hornemann."

"Yes," I said. "I'm sure the fireworks will be fun."

"And not just that," he said, "but think of the sense of history that will pervade the globe. I can almost feel it."

I held my tongue. Be kind, I said to myself, he hasn't done anything to you, it's just how he is; when he's sober he too is probably lonely and discontented, everyone is, they just don't know it, or they call it something else.

So I drained my glass and said I had to go, that I had a prior engagement.

"Well, that's how it is," he said, "you finally meet someone you know and it turns out he's busy. Still, I'm glad I recognized you."

"Goodbye," I said.

"Goodbye, Hornemann, and thanks for the chat."

When I arrived home I found a note stuck in the chink of the door. It was from my twin brother. It said, in messy writing: "I presume you're at home, even though you won't open the door. I've come to wish you a happy birthday, I don't suppose anyone else will. At least I know where you live now. I'll be back. John."

I hurried inside, locked the door and put the chain on. I didn't venture out again that day, for fear he might be lurking in the entranceway on the lookout for me.

But in the end it actually turned out to be a good day, one of the best. I had a magazine lying around that I was only halfway through. That evening I read the rest of it. One of the articles was about the recent discovery of a new quasar. It was almost 73 billion miles away and the light from it had been emitted 12.4 billion years ago – which was almost 8 billion years before our own solar system came into being, and long before the Milky Way came into existence 10 billion years ago.

Ah, now that was a lesson in perspective. I felt so elated that I opened a window to look up into space. Of course, I couldn't see anything, it's been a long time since anyone has seen a starry sky over this city, but that didn't matter much; I knew that infinity existed and all that is irrational will perish within it.

Around once a week I go to a restaurant not far from where I live. It's my regular haunt. The waiters have become used to seeing me, I'd almost go so far as to say they accept me. I sit at a small table and drink three or four pints, and that takes up a whole evening. Other regulars, having seen me there so often, sometimes say hello and I find that heartening. And, at times, someone or other will speak to me, but the person concerned is usually either so drunk he doesn't know what he's doing, or he's a pain in the neck who's been turned away from every other table and views me as a last resort. I never ask them to sit down, and if they do anyway, I make them go away.

It's a nice place to be and if I could afford to I'd go there every evening. I've often dreamt about that, being able to go every evening.

But the other day, the last time I was there, I saw to my horror my twin brother walking in. I bent down as quickly as I could and pretended to pick something up off the floor, but he'd already spotted me. I saw his feet stop right in front of me.

"Can't you find anything?" he said.

I straightened up but didn't reply. He sat down. I felt deep despair: he was going to take my local away from me.

"So this is where you hang out?" he said.

"Leave me alone," I sighed.

"Alone? Is that any way to speak to your own brother? I come here to have a chat and you tell me to leave you alone?"

"I would just rather sit on my own."

He flared up and grew very loud. How I hate him. And in my bitterness over the fact he was about to take away the last refuge I had outside my own four walls, I said:

"You're not my brother."

We'd already attracted the attention of the people sitting at the nearby tables, and what I said only made things worse. John flew into a rage, reached across the table, grabbed me by the lapel of my jacket and cried:

"Say that again!"

I didn't think that was necessary, besides I could see the waiter was approaching our table.

"I don't want any trouble here," he said.

"Would you kindly ask this man to leave," I said. "He claims he's my twin brother."

For a moment John stared at me in astonishment, then he gave me a hard shove, and at the same time released his grip on the front of my jacket. My chair tipped back and as I was on my way backwards towards the floor I thought: I'm too old to fall, I'm going to break into pieces.

But it was the chair that broke apart. I did bang the back of my head against the floor; it didn't hurt too badly but to my horror I could feel that I'd wet my trousers, and I was so ashamed that I lay for a while with my eyes closed, up until I felt a hand on my cheek. Then I looked up to see several faces. From over by the exit I heard John shouting that he was my twin brother.

"Are you alright?" one of the men standing over me asked.

"Yes, yes, thank you," I replied, confused. Then I managed a smile, an ugly one no doubt. But they helped me up, they were extremely helpful, friendly even, and I grew sentimental and thanked all around.

So I sat there as before, but with wet trousers. John had been thrown out, but was probably waiting for me outside someplace. I comforted myself with the thought that it was a while until closing time; perhaps he'd give up and postpone his revenge until some later date.

I glanced down at my lap. Oh, it was bad. A large dark stain that, try as I might, I couldn't relate to rationally. My dignity! I groaned inside myself, but of course it had nothing to do with that, but rather with my vanity.

Then a man came over to me. He was probably one of those who had stood bent over me, and must have seen me glance down despondently at my lap. He placed a jar of small salt and pepper sachets on my table and told me to sprinkle some salt on it, saying it would absorb the moisture. Imagine, such an act of kindness. I felt warm inside and was on the verge of standing up to shake his hand but was afraid he wouldn't like that, so I merely thanked him instead.

"Anyway, everyone will just think it's beer," he said.

Of course I didn't believe that, in my experience people tend to think the worst. But he meant well so I thanked him warmly for his words of comfort.

I sprinkled two sachets of salt on myself and considered how maybe it was time for me to start carrying such handy salt sachets around with me, just in case. Not to mention the pepper ones I suddenly thought, and hurriedly stuck four of them into my pocket. Ha! I thought cockily, now John can just try it!

After a while I needed to go to the washroom, and I have to say, I went there with renewed courage and my head held high. Which I shouldn't have done, I should have kept in mind that restaurant washrooms are places for all manner of discharge. I'd hardly come through the door when a drunken youth glanced at me, then did a double take and asked where they'd dug me up. I usually don't respond to that kind of thing but at that particular moment . . . well, I wasn't entirely sober, so I asked if he'd never learned any manners. He went from being rude to being nasty. He threw a number of insults at me, and the whole scene was extra excruciating because there was another man at the urinal who could hear. I said something particularly foul to the young man, I won't say what, and he came right up into my face with his small eyes. He wanted to hit me, I was sure of it, and in a way I found that reasonable, he must have been aware that, physically, he was far superior. But he contented himself with waving his fist under my nose. Just then the doorman came in. The only way he could have seen us was if the toilets were under surveillance, I never would've thought I'd view that as a good thing. At that moment I did, although my opinion was short-lived.

"Seems to be nothing but trouble with you this evening," he said. I was the one he was addressing.

"With me?" I said, stunned. "I was assaulted by him."

"Sure. First osne, and now another. That's more than enough assaults for one evening. I think it would be best if you called it a night."

I knew I'd lost, I've never heard of any bouncers changing their minds; once they've decided something, they're impervious to plain reason.

Nevertheless, because such an important part of my life was at stake I was determined to try, but I'd hardly opened my mouth before he crushed me:

"And you can stop pinching the salt and pepper sachets. You're hardly that poor."

I had no answer. There was nothing I could say that wouldn't further damage my credibility.

Oh, how I understand those who fight injustice. If he'd been smaller and I'd been younger, if only I'd had so much as a fraction of a chance of winning, I would have taken him on. Oh yes, I would have beaten him down. I still have that much truth left in me. What am I saying: truth? I mean sense of justice. No, not that either. There are too many fine words in the world. Aggression – that's the word – it's a good one.

I don't know if I actually thought all this while I was standing there, but I felt it. So I raised my fist and walked out, and that was all I did. It was all I could do. I raised my fist high above my head, like young people in protest marches do. And I walked out of the washroom and out of the restaurant, and I was sure I was walking out of there for the last time. It's not an exaggeration to say I felt great bitterness.

But I soon had other things on my mind than the world having shrunken so drastically and irrevocably. I had left the washroom without relieving myself; now the need for release arose afresh, rendering my musings on freedom quite insignificant. Ah yes, in this way too the spiritual is drowned by the physical.

But once I'd made it home and satisfied my primary needs, my bitterness returned. Or my sorrow, I might as well call it sorrow. Now you've hardly anything left to lose, Paul, I said, now you're almost done.

But when I finally fell asleep – it took a long time – I had a dream. I don't believe in dreams, or rather, I don't believe in interpreting them. All the same, a dream can make you wake up feeling refreshed, happy almost. And this dream was such that I woke with a spark of optimism. I dreamt that John was dead. I was at his funeral, and his daughter was there too. She was laughing the entire time, especially when the coffin was being lowered and it turned out to be bigger than the grave, making it impossible to get it down. His daughter was laughing so much that she was bent double and I couldn't help but laugh as well. Then she came over to me and said let's go, let's not waste any more time, I've loved you as long as I can remember, let's go back to your place. And we left, and she laughed the whole way, and touched me – it was shameless but nice. Then she pointed at the setting sun, and it suddenly jumped up in the sky, and then it rose and rose. And she was touching me the whole time, so much so that I actually woke up, and then it was morning. And at breakfast, as I was eating my egg, I said to myself: you shouldn't give up, Paul, you should go there again, you're not barred for life, and anyway that bouncer isn't there so often, he may only be covering for someone else, you shouldn't let anyone take something from you, not before they actually have. Go there again.

I don't know. It was a good dream, but it doesn't have anything to do with the restaurant. Sometimes I think about going there again and acting as if nothing happened. But that won't be easy. So I don't know. After all, it was only a dream.

Thomas F's Final Notes to the Public

Carl Lange

H E WAS STANDING by the window when a police car pulled in on the far side of the street three storeys below. Two men got out. The man by the window thought he knew where they were going, the police had often called there before.

He remained at the window to see if they took the man with them. Then the doorbell rang. It was them.

"Carl Lange?" the smaller of the two said, they were both quite large.

"Yes?"

"May we come in?"

"By all means."

He did not ask them to sit down. Nor did he take a seat himself. Their size made him feel slightly uneasy.

"Would you mind if we asked you a few questions?"

"What is it regarding?"

"Were you shopping at the Irma supermarket approximately three hours ago?"

Carl Lange looked at his watch.

"Yes?"

"Can you tell me what you were wearing?"

"The same as I have on now. And a gray three-quarter length coat. Why?"

"I'm getting to that. You're quite within your rights to refuse to answer any questions . . . for the time being."

"For the time being?"

"That's correct. What do you work as?"

"A translator. Am I accused of something?"

"No. How old are you?"

"Forty-eight."

"Would you mind telling me what you did yesterday?"

"I don't know."

"You don't know?"

"I'd like to know why you're asking."

"I understand. But your answer is more important to us if you don't know that."

"I was at home. Working."

"All day?"

"I went down to the corner shop to buy some things."

"What time was that?"

"Around ten."

"And you were at home the rest of the day? How long did you work?"

"The whole time. Until I went to bed."

"Indeed."

"What's all this about?"

"I'm getting to that. What would you say if I told you that you were seen in the vicinity of Tøyen swimming baths last night at around ten-thirty PM?"

"That it's not true."

Carl Lange looked from one of the large men to the other. Their gazes were steady, scrutinizing. The larger of the two, the one who had yet to speak, was standing with his hands behind his back. Their silence seemed threatening. Carl Lange got the feeling his own behavior was reinforcing their suspicions, so he said:

"And even if it was? If I really had been there, then so what?"

They looked at him but neither replied.

"I'd be perfectly within my rights to hang around Tøyen swimming pools at ten-thirty at night, wouldn't I?"

"Of course. Were you there?"

"No!"

"Then surely there's no reason to get so worked up. If you weren't there – well, then you weren't there. Is there anybody that can corroborate your being at home?"

"You said before I wasn't accused of anything."

"That's correct. You haven't answered the question."

"I don't intend to answer any more questions."

"That would be foolish."

"Are you threatening me?"

"A young girl was raped in the vicinity of Tøyen swimming pools at around ten-thirty last night."

Carl Lange said nothing. He wanted to say a lot of things all at once but remained standing silently while panic and anger entangled within him.

The smaller of the two large men said:

"The girl has given a good description, consisting of several distinguishing characteristics."

Carl Lange did not break his silence.

"The man was approximately forty-five years of age, had a short goatee and thick gray hair that fell down over his ears. He was wearing a light-colored pair of corduroy trousers, a brown turtleneck and a gray three-quarter length coat of a type she hadn't seen before."

Carl Lange stood in silence. He felt he looked guilty.

"Where do you keep your coat?"

Carl Lange nodded in the direction of the hallway. The larger of the men took his hands from behind his back and went to find it. Upon returning, he opened his mouth for the first time and said:

"This it?"

"Yes."

"We'd like to take it with us," the other one said. "Together with the trousers you have on. Is that alright?"

"No."

"That only makes things difficult. Then we'll have to take you along with us."

"You said I wasn't accused of anything."

"You're merely a suspect, at present. If you have nothing to hide then you should concern yourself with diminishing that suspicion. We're here to clear up a crime. There's nothing to stop us taking you in with us. We're merely offering you a choice."

Until this point Carl Lange had looked the policeman in the eye. Now he lowered his gaze, standing for a moment with eyes downcast before slowly beginning to remove his trousers. He felt an intense defiance within, but it was impotent, resigned almost, so instead of going to the bedroom and changing he undressed right in front of them. He then stood in his green briefs with the light corduroy trousers in his hand. The policeman took them without a word. Carl Lange went to the bedroom and closed the door behind him. He took his time. He found himself unable to think straight. From the living room he could hear the sound of low voices. He put on a pair of trousers almost identical to the pair he had handed over. The telephone rang. He went in to the living room and picked it up.

"Yes?"

"It's Robert. Did I catch you at a bad time?"

"I . . . are you calling from home?"

"Yes."

"Then I'll ring you back in a little while."

He replaced the receiver quickly. Then looked at the policemen and said:

"Was there anything else?"

"Not at the moment. Here's a receipt for the coat and trousers. We'll be in touch. You don't have any travel plans in the near future?"

"No."

"Try not to take this personally."

"No kidding. By the way I didn't catch your name."

"Hans Osmundsen."

"Hans Osmundsen."

He went over to the desk and wrote his name on the back of an envelope, then turned and said:

"Well, that was everything."

They left. Carl Lange stood by the window watching the car start up and drive away.

Then he went to the kitchen and looked in the mirror. He was aware he had to return a call but he put that to one side. He found the blue plastic washbasin and filled it with hot water, then went to the bathroom and fetched a safety razor and a scissors. A few minutes later his beard was gone. He looked at himself, thinking: why did I ask if I'd been shopping at Irma?

When he had rinsed the basin and returned it to the cupboard he went to make the call.

"It's Carl. I had my mother over, she was just on her way out when you called."

"Ah, of course, I understood it was something or other. Well, anyway, I was calling because I've a colleague visiting from Germany, West Germany, a nice guy who I'm sure you'd get on well with, he speaks English, but his wife is with him and she understands only German, and that's not exactly my strong suit. So I was wondering if you had the opportunity to pop by this evening – do you?"

"Now, let me think. This evening? I'm working on something with a tight deadline, you see."

"Really. That's a shame. Still, do try and make it over, Carl, if you can."

"Okay, I'll try but I'm not promising anything."

"Alright, Carl, thanks."

He put the phone down and remained standing, thinking: if they weren't bluffing about the description, why didn't they arrest me? They must have been bluffing. Or else they're giving me enough rope to see what I get up to?

Carl Lange began pacing back and forth across the not particularly lengthy floor; he went over the conversation with the policeman again, attempting to deduce the gist of what he had said. He arrived at no other conclusion than the obvious: he was suspected of having raped an underage girl.

A couple of hours later, Carl Lange left the apartment. He did not meet anyone on the stairs; if however he had, that person would have observed that he looked different. He had not only shaved off his beard; his hair was noticeably shorter and he was wearing a peaked cap he had not used in years. He was dressed in dark-colored trousers and a well-worn, almost threadbare, reefer jacket. No one who knew him would have had any difficulty in recognizing him but he looked different. The description no longer matched.

There were two reasons that Carl Lange went out. He wanted to see if the police were keeping him under surveillance, in which case he wanted to shake them. That was one reason. The other was an increasing desperation that made the apartment feel cramped: he had been fingered (at Irma? – by whom?) as a sexual offender, and two policemen had, after meeting and speaking to him, upheld that suspicion. They had met him and spoken to him, and he had not managed to convince them that he was not a sexual offender!

His first reason for going out was soon cleared up. No one was following him. With the benefit of hindsight, this became obvious to him: of course there wasn't; the police could hardly imagine that he'd go out straight away and commit another rape.

But the second reason compelled him to keep walking the streets, without being able to put any of the humiliation behind him. At one point he considered heading straight for the police station to call on this Osmundsen and tell him who he was, but he was stopped by a paralyzing counter-argument: who I am?

He did not go to Robert's place; that seemed impracticable, not least because he had altered his appearance. He pulled out the telephone lead. He tried to work but gave up. He was troubled by a memory that had cropped up while he was out roaming the streets. It was old, over twenty years old, the children had been small. They had an eight-year-old friend who liked looking after them. One afternoon he had been lying down for a rest in the bedroom, with only a light blanket over him when she came in, probably to ask about something or other. He had no recollection of what was said but while they were talking she began fiddling with one of the buttons on his shirt. This he found arousing and he got an erection. He would have liked her to stay there and fiddle not just with the shirt button but with him, it was utterly preposterous but that was how it was. This was the memory that troubled him.

He took two sleeping pills and lay awake for a long time.

Next morning he alternated between sitting and pacing about, waiting for the telephone to ring. He had no idea how long they needed to examine the clothes they had taken but he was determined not to sit around waiting indefinitely to be cleared. Better to be proactive, he thought despondently.

The telephone did not ring so he went to the police station. He felt a mixture of aggression and fear. He asked to speak to Hans Osmundsen. He had to wait. He no longer knew what he was going to say. Everything he had planned to say now either seemed meaningless or he had forgotten it.

Osmundsen, sitting back in his chair, was neither friendly nor unfriendly.

"Take a seat," he told him, but said nothing more.

"I've been waiting to hear from you," Carl Lange said.

"Oh? Why's that?"

"I want to get this business over with."

"With regard to your involvement, you mean?"

"Yes. It's not particularly pleasant to have this suspicion hanging over you."

"The examination of your clothes has yet to be completed. Not that that necessarily means anything one way or another. As I'm sure you understand."

"You mean it could serve to convict me but not to rule me out?"

"Precisely. You've shaved, I see. And cut your hair?"

Carl Lange did not reply. Osmundsen said:

"Yesterday you didn't answer as to whether you had any witnesses who could confirm that you were home the night before last."

"No."

"No what?"

"I don't have any witnesses. You don't normally have witnesses to testify to your innocence. I've never had any need of witnesses."

"You haven't?"

"No."

"Think back. To about eight years ago."

Carl Lange was taken aback, did not understand.

"I don't know what you mean," he said.

"No? On the street, on St. Olavs Gate, does that ring a bell? You were taken into custody."

"Oh, that. Yes, I remember now."

"You'd forgotten about it?"

"Yes."

"But now you remember?"

"I just said that."

"And the details, do you recall them?"

"Yes, but what's that got to do with this case?"

"Perhaps a great deal. Perhaps nothing. It's too early to say."

"Now listen here!"

"One moment, Lange. I have the police report in front of me. Let me sum up the main points. A patrol car was dispatched to 8 St. Olavs Gate in response to a call about an intoxicated girl who had lain down on the pavement to sleep. It was just before midnight and it was cold. By the time the police arrived a small crowd of eight to ten people had gathered and you were one of them. When the three officers attempted to bring the inebriated girl along with them you protested, saying she was supposed to go back to your place. You stated that she'd agreed to this and were so fiercely opposed to her being taken from you that the officers found it necessary to take you into custody. The girl was a minor."

Carl Lange sat in silence for a long time. He was stunned. Eventually he got to his feet.

"Just sit down," Osmundsen said.

Carl Lange remained standing. He stood loathing the man in front of him. He said:

"Thank you for the synopsis. I don't know whether you're the one being dishonest or the person who wrote the report. Once I've left, you might take the trouble to read my version of events, if it hasn't been shredded that is."

"I have read it."

"In that case, you must also know that I was fined for obstructing the police. And that when I refused to pay the fine, it was waived, and the case was dropped. Why was that, do you think?"

Osmundsen looked at him but said nothing.

Carl Lange continued:

"The police report stated that I was intoxicated. That was untrue and I told them the staff of the restaurant I was at could confirm that. Furthermore, it stated that I was violent and had, among other things, been involved in a scuffle with an old man with a walking stick. However, I could also prove I had a three-day-old fractured rib. I was able to pick that police report apart, bit by bit, that's why the case was dropped."

"Yes, those officers did a poor job and it was to your benefit. They considered the whole thing a trivial matter and didn't take down the names or addresses of any of the witnesses. But what are you getting so worked up for if everything you said checked out?"

"And how can you sit there so calmly when nothing you say checks out?"

"Why have you shaved off your beard and cut your hair?"

Carl Lange's first thought was to snap at him, to say it was none of his business. But he held back. Instead he said:

"Because I have an imagination."

He turned and left.

Carl Lange was at home. He paced the room. The telephone rang; he did not answer it. This was not how the world should be. The ringing continued for a long time. It might be the police, it might be anyone. He was not there. He went through his defeat at the hands of Osmundsen yet again, thinking about what he should have said. The only thing he was happy with was his parting shot. All the rest had been lacking and far too defensive.

It was not hard to understand Osmundsen's sense of triumph in being able to produce the eight-year-old case, especially when he could point to the fact that the girl had been underage, which incidentally he hadn't been aware of. He'd been walking up St. Olavs Gate that night, seen the figure lying against the cellar wall and thought it was a boy. Sleet was falling and he couldn't bring himself to just walk past. He spoke to the figure but got no response. A young couple passing by stopped. He explained that he had a fractured rib but if they managed to give the guy a shake and bring him around, he could come home with him, as he lived nearby. "It's not a he," the woman said. "It's a she." He replied that it made no difference. They managed to bring her round. She wanted to go with him. At that moment the police car arrived. He tried to explain the situation and asked if it was really necessary for them to take her in. Their brusque rejections made him angry and he told him they were behaving in a pig-headed way. That was all it took; one of the officers placed him in an armlock, the pain of which was only exacerbated by his fractured rib, and he let out a scream. He was then bundled into the car and driven to the police station at 19 Møllergata.

This was what Osmundsen had used against him. He could see the logic in it. A middle-aged man wanted to bring a drunk underage girl home with him. He understood that was how it could look, especially now. He was a suspect. A social act had, in the light of the suspicion that had arisen, become asocial, criminal.

Carl Lange found that following his visit to the police station he was less preoccupied with being under suspicion of rape than with Hans Osmundsen the person, or rather, what he stood for. Hans Osmundsen was an enemy. In Carl Lange's eyes he represented the cold, intelligent arrogance of power. His résumé of the police report had been a master class in exactly that; nothing he had said was expressly untrue but it had been thoroughly tendentious.

Carl Lange decided to pay him another visit.

However, Osmundsen called upon him instead, the following afternoon, together with the large policeman who had accompanied him previously. They had Carl's clothes with them. He did not offer them a seat even though they stood towering over him. Nor did he ask them anything. He said:

"I was actually planning on calling on you."

"That so?"

"I was surprised I haven't been presented face-to-face to the girl in question. Or her to me, rather."

"And you're saying this now, after you have changed your appearance?"

"Well, you could always procure a matching fake beard for the occasion."

"We could. But you've also cut your hair."

"I do so at regular intervals. Are you unwilling to take a chance on her not recognizing me?"

Osmundsen did not answer, instead he said:

"The girl is still in an unstable condition after what happened. Her doctor won't allow her be exposed to anything that may cause her further trauma."

Carl Lange was silent for a few moments, then he said:

"I see. So that's the reason. Why didn't you tell me that right away? Why are you toying with me?"

"Why did you shave off your beard and cut your hair?"

"I've already answered that."

"Your answer didn't make any sense to me."

"Because I didn't want to have the same appearance as a rapist."

"There are probably more clean-shaven rapists than bearded ones, just so you know."

"That wasn't a particularly intelligent comment."

For the first time, Osmundsen looked uncomfortable. There was a flicker in his eyes. But he did not respond. Carl Lange said:

"But I doubt you came all this way just to ask me that."

"We brought your clothes."

"It takes two of you to return my clothes?"

"You haven't asked about the results."

"That wouldn't be particularly smart. If I did, you might think I was unsure of whether or not you'd found something. Isn't that so?"

"So you've thought it through. You'd like to give the impression of being confident we haven't found anything?"

"Yes."

"Suppose we have found something."

"Then things would have turned out the way you wanted."

"We found traces of semen."

Carl Lange didn't reply. He didn't need to think very long to know that what Osmundsen was saying could be true and he felt himself blush with shame. He was simultaneously gripped by anger; this was his private life, an intimate matter, taboo for all but himself.

"You're very quiet," Osmundsen said.

"I don't respond to trickery. You haven't found anything of relevance to the case so just swallow the defeat. You're a pretty vile individual, but you're no doubt aware of that."

"You're getting pretty carried away. I'm trying to solve a vile crime, the vilest kind I know of."

Carl Lange knew he had over-reacted but his anger hadn't subsided and he said:

"Meaning then you're allowed resort to vile tricks?"

"I'm just telling you what we found."

"Sure. And what conclusions do you draw from that?"

"Nothing definite. But your reaction was considerably stronger than I expected."

"That doesn't surprise me. Tell me something, have you found any other suspects apart from me?"

Osmundsen merely looked at him.

"Are you even looking for anyone else? Since, as you say, you are trying to solve the vilest crime you can think of. Am I the only person in the whole of Oslo who matches the description given by a terrified girl?"

"Are you attempting to cast doubt on the description she has given?"

"You didn't answer my question."

Osmundsen was silent.

Carl Lange turned and walked to the window, stood with his back to them.

"We'll be in touch," he heard Osmundsen say. He did not turn around but heard them leave.

Carl Lange was unable to work. He brooded. He took pills to help him sleep and woke feeling sluggish. Two days passed. He brooded but got nowhere.

Then, on impulse, he looked up the number for Hans Osmundsen in the telephone directory. He simply wanted to find out his professional title. There were four people named Hans Osmundsen. Two of them had other professional titles. One of the remaining two lived in Kirkeveien, while the other had an address only four blocks away.

Something suddenly occurred to him. Suppose the one living nearby was the same Osmundsen. And suppose he was familiar with Carl's appearance from beforehand and had been the one who had seen him going in or out of the Irma supermarket, then perhaps Carl sprang immediately to mind when he heard the girl's description.

His mind was racing, his thoughts going in one direction, then the next, and he became very worked up.

He had put down the telephone directory, but now he opened it again and looked up the name and number. He decided to call and find out if he was right. But he changed his mind, had no wish to get in touch with the policeman, and was not sure what he would say if he did. Instead he rang the number in Kirkeveien. If that address could be eliminated, which he was almost certain it could, then that would settle it. A policeman had to have a home telephone.

But his certainty did not prevent him placing a handkerchief over the mouthpiece, giving him the feeling of doing something illegal.

A woman answered on the other end. He asked if he had come to the residence of Inspector Osmundsen. He had not. He apologized and put the phone down.

He put on the gray overcoat, for the first time since getting it back, and went out. He was excited. He walked four blocks west and found the address, a newly renovated, four-storey apartment building. As he suspected: the shortest route from Osmundsen's home to the police station ran past the Irma supermarket.

But how had Osmundsen tracked *him* down? Had he simply followed him to the entrance of his building, before giving his description to other tenants and finding out which flat he lived in?

Carl Lange did not halt outside Osmundsen's apartment building, nor did he go in. He walked on for a few hundred meters, turned a corner and took another route home. He did not want to be seen. Once again he had the distinct impression of doing something illegal.

On the stairs up to his apartment he ran into Osmundsen on the way down, alone. Carl Lange was in his own thoughts and caught off guard.

"There you are," Osmundsen said.

He did not reply.

"Can I come up?"

"What is it you want now?"

"To talk to you."

Carl Lange did not say anything else but continued up the stairs and Osmundsen followed. He unlocked the door, went into the living room without removing his coat, and sat down. Osmundsen took a seat as well.

Carl Lange felt a sudden calm descend, as though everything he had been ruminating upon over the last few days had now sprouted, making him invulnerable. He said:

"How long have you known me? Or perhaps I should say: known about me?"

"What do you mean by that?"

"I don't expect you to answer. Well, what was it you wanted?"

"I'm here regarding the matter of that identity parade we spoke about."

"I'm no longer interested."

"I think you misunderstand. *We* are interested."

He made no reply. He felt quite composed. He waited but so did Osmundsen; as though they were duelling, with silence as the weapon of choice.

Carl Lange was first to give in, but he remained calm, feeling almost as if he had the upper hand:

"How many suspects have you come up with?"

"You asked me that the last time too."

"And you didn't answer. Perhaps you're not particularly adept at lying?"

"No. Are you?"

"Yes, when it's appropriate. Who was it that saw me at Irma?"

"And when is it appropriate?"

Carl Lange stood up, removed his coat and draped it over the back of a chair before sitting back down, only this time with his face and body turned slightly away.

Osmundsen said:

"You were married, weren't you?"

"That's right."

"But you divorced around eight years back."

"So you know about that."

"Yes. From what I understand you were the one who filed for divorce."

"Where did you hear that?"

"Was that not the case? You left home abruptly, saying you were depressed and needed to be by yourself for a while. A few days later you phoned saying you wanted to end the marriage."

Osmundsen paused. Carl Lange said nothing but his earlier calmness had been swept away.

"You have to admit," Osmundsen continued, "it was an unusual way to end a marriage, even in this day and age. But perhaps you had your motives and didn't want your wife to know about them?"

Carl Lange remained sitting, his face turned away from Osmundsen. Trying to adopt an indifferent tone, he said:

"And what motives might they have been?"

"Well, to keep another relationship secret, for instance."

"Why?"

"Why indeed."

Carl Lange couldn't take any more. Here was a man who, by virtue of his professional position, could take the liberty of poking around in his affairs, of sticking his nose into his private and emotional life, it was humiliating. Gripped by a feeling of intense defiance, he rose to his feet, he did not know what to do, but he could not take any more, and almost without being aware of it he just walked away, out of the living room, out of the apartment, down the stairs, unhurriedly at first, then at a gallop, while thinking: now he definitely thinks I'm guilty. But that did not bother him, on the contrary, leading Osmundsen on a wild goose chase was retaliation of a sort.

On reaching the corner of the street, he looked back. No sign of Osmundsen. He kept up a brisk pace until he felt safe, then went into a small café where there were hardly any customers. He took a seat by the window and ordered a waffle and a coffee.

He tried to calm down but was unable. He pictured Osmundsen, the level-headed and at the same time underhand, crafty Osmundsen, who sat cold and detached, prodding him with all his malicious insinuations. How he loathed him, how he abhorred him!

Two hours later he let himself into his apartment. He was still agitated so he took a sleeping pill to calm himself. It was half past three. He paced back and forth waiting for the pill to work. Noticing no effect after half an hour, he took one more. Just then the telephone rang. He did not take it. He paced the room, but never went close enough to the window to be seen from outside. Then, remembering Osmundsen had mentioned the identity parade, he picked up the coat from over the chair, went into the bedroom to fetch a pair of scissors, then sat down on the sofa and began cutting the coat to shreds. He placed the strips in a plastic bag. He had grown calm. I could of course have hidden it someplace, he thought. He lay down on the sofa and pulled a blanket over himself. I'll soon have lost almost a week's wages, he thought, this can't go on, I need to get back to work.

The doorbell rang. He froze, listened, but heard only the pumping of his own blood. There was another ring, longer, more impatient, he thought. I'm quite within my rights not to open, he thought, after all, I'm not even sure who it is. But I must get a more secure lock.

He remained lying on the sofa, waited for a few minutes, before getting up and creeping like a thief into the hallway and to the door. He put his ear against it, heard nothing but did not dare open to make sure, not yet. He returned to the living room, took out a writing block with blank pages and wrote: "Gone to cabin in Hallingdal to do some work in peace and quiet. Back in about two weeks." Then he folded the sheet and wrote *Robert* on the back. He opened the odds-and-ends drawer, found a thumbtack, went back to the front door, listened, then opened it and pinned the message below the doorbell. Smart, Carl, he said to himself, feeling buoyed. But after a while it occurred to him that of course Robert knew he had no cabin in Hallingdal, and he wrote a new note: "Gone to a cabin I've borrowed in Hallingdal to get some work done in peace and quiet. I'll be in touch." And on the outside of the folded sheet he wrote *Sylvia*, safe in the knowledge that no Sylvia would ever come calling. Now I'm no longer here, he thought.

But then it occurred to him that he needed to stock up on food so he hurried down to the corner shop.

Once safely back home again, he drew the curtains across one of the two windows facing the street and switched on the lamp beside the sofa. The dim light would no doubt be visible from outside but it was quite common nowadays to safeguard against burglary by not leaving an empty apartment to lie in complete darkness over a prolonged period. Now I'm no longer here, he thought once more, and settled down on the sofa. Feeling tired, he lay down, pulled the blanket over him, and as sleep washed over him like long, calm swells, he thought: I must remember to pin the note in such a way so as to see if Osmundsen has read it.

He woke disoriented. He was cold. It was night and dark, the time was ten past five, and he had slept for over twelve hours. He undressed and went to lie down in the bedroom. He fell back asleep and dreamt that he wrote a postcard to himself saying he was in France, and he put a Norwegian and a French stamp on the card. He was awoken by the dream. It was still dark. This time he did not fall back asleep. He lay thinking about the measures he had taken the previous day; they suddenly seemed quite baffling; he must have had some motive he was unable to grasp. But one thing gradually became alarmingly obvious to him: from the moment Osmundsen had informed him he was under suspicion, it had, no matter how unfounded, influenced, if not directly steered, his entire way of being. Prior to that he had viewed himself as a relatively free, relatively autonomous individual, even though he was of course aware that he was not immune from common social influences. However he now lay there feeling that someone else's will, that of Osmundsen, was constantly pushing him into new situations where his reactions were constrained and consequently irrational.

Carl Lange sequestered himself for two days. The telephone rang five times. That was a good deal more often than usual. It could of course have been his mother. Or one of the children. Or someone else. Carl Lange believed it was Osmundsen.

He slept a lot, took pills and grew sleepy. When he was awake, especially just prior to falling asleep, he played out conversations with Osmundsen. Initially he himself did most of the talking; accusing Osmundsen of stripping him of his identity. But gradually Osmundsen got more lines and he could say things that made Carl Lange livid with rage. At one point he said: "You're filth, a louse, devoid of social conscience. Crushing you will be a pleasure."

On the third day, a Sunday, he called Osmundsen on his home number, figuring he would be off work. He was, and answered the phone himself.

"Yes?"

"It's Carl Lange."

A brief pause, then:

"Yes?"

"I've been away for a couple of days."

"Oh?"

"I wondered if there was anything new, if you had perhaps tried to get in touch with me?"

"Get in touch with you?"

"Just answer me!"

"Take it easy, Lange. So you think I'm the one who's been calling while you were away?"

"What do you mean?"

"Now you're making both you and me out to be more stupid than we are. You were in Hallingdal, you said?"

"I didn't say . . ."

"It's all right, Lange. Telling lies is permissible every place but in court, and even there the accused is allowed do it. But can't you call me tomorrow instead, I'm just on my way out."

Carl Lange slammed down the phone without responding, he had no response. He was humiliated, had been made a fool of, ridiculed. Bastard, he cursed inwardly, that fucking bastard.

He took two pills. What am I doing, he thought afterwards. What is he doing to me?

He paced the floor furiously for a half hour until the pills began to take effect. Then sat down, calmer, but at a loss. He knew I was at home the entire time, he knows where I am the entire time. He genuinely thinks I did it, despite all our conversations.

He got to his feet and began pacing again, remembered the note outside on the door, and went to take it down. He could not see any sign that it had been touched. "You were in Hallingdal, you said?"

He took another pill, wanted to sleep, wanted to get away, even though it was still only the afternoon. He lay down and tried to work out what he was going to say to Osmundsen the next day but his thoughts were swimming in a kind of haze and he could not hold on to them. Fatigue rolled over him like long, heavy waves, and within them Osmundsen's face, coming and going, a calm, grave face.

Carl Lange struggled to wake up. He knew in his sleep that it was a dream: he was standing on an enormous glacier, by a narrow fissure, the bottom of which he could not see. He was going to throw himself down it, he had strove for a long time to find precisely this rift in the ice, which would hide him forever. But he was now paralyzed by a terrible doubt: he could not remember where he had left the message that said should anything happen to him then it was his neighbor, the one who had often threatened to kill him, who was the guilty party. No one would think his neighbor was capable of doing it but, he had written, he had been. But now he did not know anymore whether the message would be found, in which case the whole thing was meaningless, the crack in front of him was meaningless, him never being found was meaningless. But the nightmare itself, what he was fighting to awaken from, was the endless rumination over what he had done with the message.

It was late afternoon. The dream had lingered as though it were more than a dream.

I'm not calling, he thought. He's waiting for me to call so I'm not going to.

But shortly afterwards he thought: but maybe he figures that's exactly the way my mind works.

Shortly after that again he put on the worn-out reefer jacket and peaked cap and set out for the police station. He had nothing prepared, not one complete sentence, not one coherent thought. All the same, he walked quickly.

He said who he was and whom he wanted to see. He had to wait. Of course, he thought, that's his tactic, I'll no doubt be waiting even longer today. But he was not; he was actually rather disappointed when he was shown through after only a few minutes. He dupes me the whole time, he said to himself, and for a moment considered turning around to leave.

Osmundsen was sitting at his desk. In a lofty manner, Carl Lange thought.

"I've been expecting you," Osmundsen said.

"I'm sure you have. You always expect what's going to happen, don't you?"

"No, unfortunately."

"Of course you do. And that's the reason you don't think I'm guilty either. You never have."

"And what of it? I don't necessarily believe a suspect to be guilty. Being under suspicion means to be within a certain scope. It can be wide or narrow."

"And I'm within that scope because you want me to be."

"You yourself have contributed to that to a large degree."

"On account of certain characteristics, as you put it."

"No. Actually the first time I paid you a visit was in order to eliminate you from our inquiries. But you seemed guilty in some way, and moreover, strikingly insensitive to the very crime. Why you've done your utmost since to cast suspicion on yourself, only you know."

"I did as the situation forced me."

"What situation? Either you were innocent or you were guilty?"

"I mean to say: as you forced me."

"You must be extremely insecure."

"Can't you ever follow the thread of a conversation," Carl Lange exploded, "must you always suddenly change the subject!"

"Oh, the thread of the conversation couldn't be clearer, but I'd be more than happy to spell it out for you. You claim that you've been pressured into acting strangely, like this latest episode about pretending you had taken a trip to Hallingdal. My response to you would be that if you, even if you say you're innocent, allow yourself to be pressured into that kind of thing, it must be down to insecurity. I could, for that matter, put it in even stronger terms. I have the impression that you are unable to decide who you are."

"What nonsense, what a load of . . . I mean, really, so now in addition to everything else you want to make out that I'm insecure and don't know who I am! No doubt I'll be of unsound mind next!"

Carl Lange had got to his feet; he felt a surge of uncontrollable anger and before he knew it he had leaned over the desk and spat on Osmundsen. Granted, it didn't hit him right in the face but on the chest. Upon realizing what he had done, he took two quick steps back in shock. He opened his mouth but found nothing to say that could express the burning shame he felt.

Osmundsen had been sitting quite motionless, as though frozen fast. He took out a handkerchief and first wiped the spray from his face and then the globule of spittle itself from his V-neck. He looked up at Carl Lange with an odd, almost absent-minded, expression.

"I . . ." Carl Lange began, but got no further.

Osmundsen didn't say anything but dropped the handkerchief on the floor beside him.

"I lost control," Carl Lange said. "I apologize."

Osmundsen nodded almost imperceptibly; Carl Lange did not know what it meant.

"You are aware that what you just did is a criminal offence."

Carl Lange did not reply; he was utterly indifferent to that aspect of the matter.

"Sit down," Osmundsen said.

"I'd prefer to stand."

"I'd prefer you sat down."

Carl Lange remained on his feet.

"Okay, as you wish," Osmundsen said. "Lucky for you there were no witnesses to what you did."

"I wasn't planning on denying it."

"Good."

Osmundsen did not say any more; a long silence ensued. Carl Lange was fast recovering from the shame of his disgraceful behavior; indeed he stood almost feeling proud for not complying with Osmundsen's order to sit. If only I had struck him instead of spitting, he thought. If the desk hadn't been in the way I would have hit him, I only spat because it was the only thing I could do.

"Well, was there anything else?" Osmundsen asked.

Carl Lange was taken aback. Well, he thought, is there anything else?

"Not at this point, no" he said, "there isn't anything else."

He turned and left, just about managing to conceal a smile. But as he made his way through the police station his smile broadened. And when he got outside under the overcast sky he laughed, inwardly admittedly, but almost out loud. I spat at him, he thought, feeling exhilarated, that was all that was needed, right there in the police station, the first punishable offence I've ever committed, that was all that was needed, and now he can't do anything to me anymore.

But his feeling of elation was short-lived, after a few minutes the final victory did not seem so final any longer. And when Carl Lange arrived home he felt an intense emptiness. He sat down still wearing his coat and hat and felt like a stranger, without ties. Now I'm finished, he thought. There is nothing else.

Chess

THE WORLD isn't like it used to be. For one thing, it takes longer to live. I'm in my late eighties, and that's still not enough. I'm far too healthy even though I've nothing more to be healthy for. But life won't let go of me. He who has nothing to live for has nothing to die for. Maybe that's why.

One day, long ago, before my legs became too frail, I went to see my brother. I hadn't seen him in over three years but he was still living in the same place. "Are you alive," he asked, even though he was older than me. I'd brought a packed lunch and he gave me a glass of water. "Life's hard," he said, "unbearable." I ate and didn't answer. I hadn't come to have a discussion. So I finished my food and drank my water. He sat staring fixedly at a point in the air above my head. If I'd stood up and he'd continued to stare, he'd have been looking directly at me. Then again he'd probably have shifted his gaze. He didn't enjoy my company. Or to be more precise, he didn't enjoy himself in my company. I think he had a guilty conscience, not a clear one, in any case. He's written twenty or so thick novels, I've written only a few, and thin ones at that. He's considered quite a good author, although salacious.

He writes a lot about love, mostly of the physical kind, wherever he gets that from.

He continued staring above my head, he probably felt entitled to, with twenty novels propping up his bloated behind, and I felt like cutting my losses and leaving, but that would have been silly after such a long walk, so I asked if he'd like a game of chess. "It takes such a long time," he said, "I don't have that much time left. You could have come sooner." I should have stood up and left at that point, it would have served him right, but I'm too polite and considerate, it's my great weakness, or one of them. "It won't take more than an hour," I said. "The game itself, yes," he replied, "but the subsequent exhilaration, or exasperation should I lose. My heart, you see, it's no longer what it was. Nor is yours I'd imagine." I made no reply, having no desire to discuss my heart on his terms. So I countered: "So you're afraid of dying. Oh well." "Hogwash. It's just that my lifework is not finished." That was exactly how he put it, his pomposity was sickening. My walking stick was on the floor and I bent down to pick it up, I'd had enough and wanted to call a halt to his boasting. "Death puts a stop to us contradicting ourselves at any rate," I said, although I didn't expect him to understand what I was referring to. But he was too high and mighty to ask what I meant. "I didn't mean to offend you," he said. "Offend me," I repeated quite loudly – I was understandably rather irked – "I don't give a damn about what little I've written and what little I haven't written." I got to my feet and delivered quite the little speech for him: "Not an hour passes without the world ridding itself of thousands of idiots. Think about it, have you considered how much stored idiocy disappears in the course of a day? All those brains ceasing to function, because that's where all the stupidity resides. And still so much stupidity is left, because someone has written it down in books, and that's how it's kept alive, as long as people read novels there will be lots of stupidity – certain novels, the majority of them." And then I added, perhaps rather vaguely, I have to admit: "which is why I came to play a game of chess." He sat silently for a while, right up until I was leaving, then he said: "That was a lot of words, serving little purpose. But I'll do what I can with them, I'll use them, I'll put them in the mouth of an ignoramus."

That was my brother for you. Incidentally, he died the same day. I was more than likely the one to hear his last words, because I left without replying, which no doubt he didn't like. He wanted to have the last word of course, and he got it, but he probably would have liked to say more. When I recall how worked up he was, I can't help but think that the Chinese have a dedicated character for dying of exhaustion during intercourse.

We were brothers after all.

Carl

W HEN MY WIFE was alive, I used to think about how much more room I'd have when she died. Just imagine all her underwear, I thought, three dresser drawers full, where I could have space for my copper coins in one, my matchboxes in another, and my corks in the third. As it is now, I thought, everything is just a mess.

Then she did die, a long time ago now. She was a demanding person, but God rest her soul, she finally gave me peace. I emptied drawers, shelves, and cupboards of her belongings, making lots of empty space, more than I could use. And what is empty is empty. So I smashed up a couple of cupboards. But that left me with an emptier room instead of two empty cupboards. It was a rather rash thing to do but, as I said, it was a long time ago, and I was a lot younger then.

Anyway, a few weeks or maybe months after carrying out this ill-considered extension of the room's emptiness, I received a surprise visit from my second-oldest son Carl. He was looking for a shawl his mother had owned, wanted to give it to his wife as a memento of his child-hood. On discovering I'd thrown it out, he became cross. "Is nothing sacred to you?" he yelled. And this coming from him – a businessman who makes his living from buying and selling. I felt like cutting him short, but held my peace, after all, I am complicit in bringing him into existence. "What was so special about this shawl?" I asked instead, in a conciliatory tone. "Mom crocheted it while she was expecting me. She was particularly fond of it." "Ah, I see. It came into being at the same time as you. You were perhaps her favorite son?" "I was, as it happens, yes." "Oh, it hardly just happened," I replied, beginning to lose patience with him, he was the spitting image of her and just as incapable of recognizing the natural order of things. "Well, the shawl is gone for good," I said. "You can take comfort in knowing that only what is lost can be possessed forever." Drivel of course, but I thought it would appeal to him. However, I was wrong. I had forgotten for a moment that he was, after all, a businessman. He took an almost threatening step toward where I was sitting, and launched into an angry but boring tirade about my insensitivity. He concluded by saying that at times he couldn't understand how I could be his father. "Your mother was a respectable woman," I replied, but he didn't catch my point – why did I have such slow-witted children? "You don't need to tell me that," he said. His face had grown quite red by this stage and it suddenly struck me that he might have a weak heart, he was sixty years old after all, and to avert possible misfortune I said I was sorry about the shawl and that had he come sooner he could have gotten everything his mother left behind. I still believe that this was a very conciliatory thing to say, but his face grew even redder. "You mean you've thrown out everything?"

he shouted. "Everything," I replied. "But why?" I didn't want to tell him so I said: "You'd never understand." "What an inhuman thing to do." "Quite the contrary. I made a conscious decision and acted upon it, which is practically the only thing that makes us specifically human." It was of course pure semantics on my part but he didn't even seem to have heard what I said. "Then there's no reason for me to be in this house," he shouted, he had gotten into the habit of shouting, indicating perhaps that his wife had gone deaf, personally I have extremely good hearing, it can be a downright nuisance at times, certain noises have become a lot louder than they used to be, as well as which completely new ones have come along, from pneumatic drills and suchlike, I wouldn't mind being deaf. "I hear what you're saying," I said, "but don't see any follow-through." Then he finally left, and about time, otherwise my patience might have run out. That said I do have more patience than I used to, it's old age I suppose, old people put up with a lot.

My Goodness

ONE SUMMER, on a day it wasn't raining, I felt like getting some exercise, taking a walk around the block, at least. The thought cheered me up, I suddenly felt in better humor than I had in a long time. The weather was so warm that I thought I'd change into short underpants, but when I went to look for them I remembered having thrown them out in a fit of melancholy the year before. But the idea of short underpants had taken hold, so I cut the legs off the ones I was wearing. You never get too old to quit hoping.

It was strange to be outside after such a long time, although naturally I recognized my surroundings. I'm going to write about this, I thought, and suddenly became aware of a growing erection, right there on the pavement, but it didn't matter because my trousers had deep, roomy pockets.

When I made it to the first corner – it took time, the spirit was willing but my legs were weak – I decided I didn't want to walk around the block after all. Since it was summer, I wanted to see some greenery, a tree at the very least, so I continued straight ahead. It was hot, as hot as when I was a child, and I was thankful for the short underpants. And with my erection deftly under control, I felt fine. That might sound like an exaggeration, but that's how it was.

When I had walked almost three buildings along I heard someone call my name. Even though it was an old voice I didn't turn around, so many people are named Thomas. But the third time I heard it I looked in the direction the voice was coming from – it was such an unusual day, anything could happen. And indeed, on the pavement opposite stood old Lector Storm. "Felix," I shouted, but I was so unaccustomed to using my voice that it wasn't much of a shout. We had a lot of traffic between us and neither he nor I dared to cross the street, it would have been stupid to lose my life from joy when I had managed to survive so long without it. So the only thing I could do was shout his name once more and wave my cane. It was a big disappointment, but he'd seen me and called my name and that was some consolation, despite everything. "Goodbye, Felix," I called out, and began to walk on.

But when I finally made it to the next crossing he was suddenly standing there right in front of me, so I'd been feeling sorry for nothing. "Thomas, my old friend," he said, "where in the world have you been?" I didn't want to tell him so instead I said: "The world is large, Felix." "And everyone is dead or almost dead." "Yes, life takes its toll." "Well said, Thomas, well said." I didn't think it in the least bit well said, and so in some kind of effort to merit his praise, I said: "As long as we cast a shadow, there's life." "You're not wrong, there's no end to evil." That was when I began to wonder if he'd gone senile, and I decided to test him. "Evil isn't the problem," I said, "but foolishness, take young men on large motorcycles for instance." He looked at me for a while, then he said: "I'm not sure I quite understand what you mean." I'd no desire to rub his face in it, so I casually remarked: "Well, what is evil?" He was of course at a loss, he was not a theologian after all, and I hastened to add: "But let's not talk about that – how are you?" I'd obviously put him in a bad mood, because he studied his watch for a long time, then said: "I become more and more lonely with every person I meet." It was not a particularly nice thing to say but I pretended not to notice. "Yes," I said, "that's how it is." I realized that if I didn't hurry up and say goodbye, he'd beat me to it, but I wasn't fast enough and he did: "But I've got to be getting on, Thomas, I have potatoes on the boil." "Of course, the potatoes," I replied. Then I put out my hand and said: "Well, if we don't see each other again—" I let the words hang in the air, it was exactly the kind of sentence that was best left unfinished. "Yes," he said and shook my hand. "Goodbye, Felix." "Goodbye, Thomas."

I turned and walked home. I hadn't seen any greenery, but my goodness, what an eventful day.

Café-goers

ONE OF THE last times I went to a café was on a Sunday in summer, I remember it well because nearly everyone was without a jacket and tie, and I thought: perhaps it isn't Sunday after all? The fact I thought that is the reason I remember it. I was at a table in the middle of the premises, and around me a lot of people were sitting eating cakes and open sandwiches, mostly one to a table. It looked quite lonely, and since I hadn't talked to anyone in a good while I was of a mind to do so, if only to exchange a few words. I thought long and hard about how to bring this about, but the more I looked at the faces around me the harder it seemed, as though everyone's eyes were unseeing. The world really has become a depressing place. But I'd gotten the idea into my head of how nice it would be if someone said a few words to me, so I kept thinking, it's the only thing that helps. And after a while I knew what to do. I dropped my wallet onto the floor, acting as though it happened unintentionally. It lay beside my chair, visible to several of those sitting nearby, and I saw many sidelong glances in its direction. I had thought that one or maybe two of them would have gotten to their feet to pick it up and hand it to me – I am an old man, after all – or at the very least call out to me, say something along the lines of: "Excuse me, you dropped your wallet." If only we could stop hoping, just think of the many disappointments we'd be spared. Finally, after several minutes of sidelong glances and waiting, I pretended to suddenly discover I'd lost it, I didn't dare wait any longer, was afraid one of those people looking at the wallet out of the corners of their eyes was going to jump up, pounce on it and make for the door. After all, no one could be sure how much money was in there, old people aren't always poor, sometimes they're even rich, that's the way of the world: those who steal when they're young or in their prime are rewarded for it in their old age.

So that's how café-goers are these days, I learned that much, you live and learn, whatever good that might be, right before you die.

Maria

ONE AUTUMN DAY I happened to run into my daughter Maria on the pavement outside the watchmaker's shop; she'd grown thinner but I'd no difficulty recognizing her. I can't remember what I was doing outdoors, but it must have been something important, because it was after the banisters on the staircase had broken, so I had actually stopped going out. Anyway I met her, and even though I know better, for a moment I thought: what a strange coincidence that I should go out on today of all days. She seemed happy to see me, because she said, "Father," and shook my hand. She was the one I used to like best of all my children, and when she was small she'd often tell me I was the best father in the world. Then she'd sing for me, out of tune it must be said, but through no fault of her own, she got that from her mother. "Maria," I said, "is it really you, you look so well." "Yes, I'm drinking urine and eating raw vegetables," she replied. I couldn't help but laugh, and it'd been a long time since I had. To think I had a daughter with a sense of humor, a slightly cheeky sense of humor at that. Who would have thought? It was a special moment. But I was mistaken, you're never too old to be stripped of your illusions. My daughter gaped at me and the light in her eyes seemed to fade. "You're making fun of me," she said, "but you've no idea." "I thought you said urine," I replied, which was the truth. "Yes, that's right, urine, I'm like a different person." I didn't doubt that, it made sense, you couldn't possibly be the same person once you started drinking urine. "I see," I said, in a conciliatory tone, I wanted to change the subject, maybe talk about something pleasant, you never know. Then I noticed she was wearing a ring, and I said: "You're married, I see." She looked at the ring. "Oh, that," she said, "I only wear it to keep pushy men from making advances." Now that *had* to be a joke, I quickly calculated that she must be at least fifty-five, and she didn't look *that* good. So I laughed again, for the second time in a long while, and in the middle of a sidewalk at that. "What are you laughing at?" she asked. "I think I must be getting old," I replied, when I realized I'd been mistaken yet again. "So that's how it's done these days." She didn't answer that, so I don't know, but I hope and presume my daughter is not particularly representative. But why did I get children like this? Why?

We stood for a moment in silence, and I was thinking it was time to say goodbye, an unexpected meeting shouldn't last too long, but then she asked if I was in good health. I'm not sure what she meant but I told her the only thing wrong with me were my legs, which was the truth. "They won't take me where I want to go any longer, my steps are getting shorter and shorter, soon I won't be able to budge an inch." I don't know why I went on to her so much about my legs, and as it turned out, it was stupid of me. "Age, I suppose," she said. "Of course it's age," I said, "what else would it be?" "But I guess you won't need to use them much longer." "Really," I said, "is that so?" She picked up on the irony, to her credit, and got annoyed, but not at herself, because she said: "Everything I say is wrong." I had no answer to that, what could I have said, instead I swayed my head in an intentionally noncommittal way, there are far too many words in circulation, the more you say the greater your chances of being wrong.

"Well, I'd better be going," my daughter said after a pause that was brief, but long enough, "I have to get to an herb shop before it closes. See you." She held out her hand. "Goodbye, Maria," I said. Then she left. That was my daughter. I know everything has its own inherent logic, but it isn't always easy to spot.

Mrs. M

ONE OF THE few people who know I still exist is Mrs. M at the corner shop. Twice a week she brings me what I need to live – she doesn't overexert herself. I seldom see her, as she has a key to the apartment and leaves the shopping inside the door; it's best that way, we protect ourselves and each other while maintaining a peaceful, almost friendly, relationship.

But one day when I heard her let herself in, I had to call out to her. I'd fallen, banged my knee, and couldn't make it to the couch. Luckily it happened on one of the days she brings the groceries, so I didn't need to wait more than four hours. She wanted to fetch the doctor immediately, and she meant well, only close relatives call the doctor out of spite, when they want to get rid of old people. I explained to her everything she needed to know about hospitals and one-way tickets to old people's homes, and compassionate person that she was, she wrapped my knee. Then she made three open sandwiches that she placed on a table by the bed, along with a decanter of water. Finally she brought in an old milk jug she'd found in the kitchen, *in case the need arises*, as she put it.

Then she left. Later that evening I was eating one of the sandwiches when she came to check on me. It was so unexpected, I have to admit my emotions got the better of me, and I said: "You're such a good person." "There, there," she replied, and began changing the dressing on my knee. "This is going to be all right," she said, and added, "so you don't want to go to an old people's home? You do know, by the way, that they're not called that any longer, now they're known as assisted living facilities." We both had a good laugh at that, the mood became almost upbeat, it's such a joy to meet people with a sense of humor.

My leg was sore for nearly a week and she came to check on me every day. On the last day I said: "I'm well again now, thanks to you." "No need to be so serious," she interrupted, "everything has gone just as it should." I agreed with her about the last part but insisted that without her my life could have taken an unfortunate turn. "Oh, you would have managed somehow," she replied, "you're so stubborn. My father was the same, so I know what I'm talking about." I felt she was drawing conclusions on a rather flimsy basis, she didn't know me after all, but I didn't want to appear reproachful so I just said: "I'm afraid you have too high an opinion of me." "Oh, not at all," she replied. "If you'd only known him, he was an extremely obstinate and difficult man." She said this in all seriousness, and I have to admit I was impressed, I felt like laughing with joy, but I maintained my composure and said: "I see. And did your father also live to be very old?" "Oh yes, very old. He was constantly disparaging about life, but I don't know anyone who struggled more against letting go of it." I could safely smile at that; it was liberating, I even chuckled, as did she. "You're probably just the same," she said, and then, out of the blue, asked if she could read my palm. I held out my hand, I don't remember which, but it was the other one she wanted. She studied it for a while, then smiled and said, "Just as I thought. You should have been dead long ago."

The Banister

A FEW MONTHS AGO I received a visit from the new landlord. He rang three times before I managed to open, even though I walked as quickly as I could. I didn't know it was him, after all. It's seldom anyone comes by, and almost all who do are representatives of religious sects asking if I've been saved. That does amuse me a little, but I never let them in, people who believe in eternal life aren't rational, you never know what they could get up to. Anyway, on this occasion it was the landlord who called. I'd written to him almost a year previously to draw his attention to the fact that the banisters on the staircase were broken, and thinking that was why he'd come, I let him in. He looked around. "Nice place you've got here," he said, and this was such a tendentious statement I realized I had to be on my guard. "The banister is broken," I said. "Yeah, I noticed, were you the one who broke it?" "No, why would it have been me?" "There're only young people living in the other apartments, so you're probably the only person who uses it, and it hardly broke itself, did it?" He was obviously a difficult person and I didn't want to enter into a discussion about the whys and wherefores of things being broken, so I said rather curtly: "Be that as it may, I need to use that banister, and have a right to do so." He didn't respond to that, however he did say the rent would increase by twenty per cent as of next month. "Again?" I said, "and by twenty per cent, that's quite a lot." "It should be more," he replied, "I'm losing money on this building." It's been a long time – must be almost thirty years – since I stopped discussing finance with people who say they're losing money on things they could get rid of, so I didn't say anything. But he didn't need any input from me to go on, he was the type who required no help from any-one else. He went on at length about all his other buildings that were also operating at a loss, it was quite the lament to listen to, he must have been a pretty lousy capitalist. But I didn't say anything and eventually his moaning came to an end, and not before time. Instead, without any apparent reason, he asked if I believed in God. I was on the verge of asking which God he was referring to but contented myself with shaking my head. "But you must," he said. So I'd let one of them into the apartment after all. Not that I was that surprised, it's not unusual for people with a lot of property to believe in God. However, having relegated evangelists to a crack in the door long ago, I wasn't going to let him get started on a new topic, so I didn't let him get any further. "So the rent is increasing by twenty per cent," I said, "I gather that's what you came to tell me." My rebuff seemed to surprise him, because he opened and closed his mouth twice without making a sound, some-thing I'd imagine was out of character for him. "And I hope you see to it that the banister is repaired," I continued. His face turned red. "The banister, the banister," he said impatiently, "you won't let up about that banister." I thought that was a stupid thing to say and became rather worked up. "But don't you understand," I said, "that on occasion that banister is all I have to hold onto in life?" I immediately regretted having said it, precise formulations should be directed at contemplative people, otherwise things become a right mess. Which they did. I can't be bothered repeating what he said, but mostly it concerned the afterlife. Finally he started talking about being at death's door, and I was the one he was referring to, so that made me angry. "Stop pestering me about your finances," I said, because really that was what this entire thing was all about, and when he didn't decide to leave right away, I took the liberty of banging on the floor once with my cane. Then he left. It was a relief, I felt happy and unencumbered for several minutes afterward, and I remember saying to myself, inwardly of course: Don't give up, Thomas, don't give up.

The Disturbance

WHEN READING or occupied with solving chess problems, I'll often sit by the window looking out. You never know when something worth watching might happen, although it's pretty unlikely, the last time was three or four years ago. But the mundane can also provide some diversion, and at least outside the window there's always something moving, in here it's only me and the hand of the clock.

But three or four years ago I did see something strange, and that was the last remarkable thing I've seen, although as I said I'm not indifferent to more everyday occurrences, people fighting for instance, hitting and kicking one another, or people keeling over on the pavement and lying there because they're either too drunk or sick to make their way home, if they have a home that is, many of them probably don't, there aren't enough homes in the world.

But what I saw that time was different. It must have been at Easter or Whitsuntide, because it wasn't in winter, and I remember thinking such an occurrence most likely had some connection to one of the religious festivals.

My window looks down upon a side street; it's not too long and I can see to the end of it without difficulty, I have good eyesight.

I was sitting following two flies mating on the windowsill, so in all probability it was at Whitsuntide; watching them provided some diversion, although they hardly moved. Looking at them didn't arouse me, not like I can remember it doing when I was young – oh yes, I remember that well.

Anyway, I was watching the two flies – I'd just touched one of the female's wings very carefully, and then one of the male's wings, without them seeming to notice, and it struck me as odd that their preoccupation with each other should be so intense, since the male had been sitting on top of the female for at least ten minutes, and that's no exaggeration. I should have spent more of my life studying insects, then again what would have been the point? – when I caught sight of a man at the far end of the street behaving in a most conspicuous manner. He was sort of flapping his arms, and shouting something, although I couldn't catch what it was in the beginning. He did move in a systematic way, although his sense of geographical organization was peculiar, because he walked, or jogged rather, from the first window on the right-hand side of the street to the first window on the left-hand side, and from there to the second window on the right-hand side then on to the second window on the left-hand side, and so on, knocking on all the doors and shouting something. It was unusual and strange, and I opened the window – this was before the hinges broke – and heard him shout: "Jesus has come." But he called out something else as well, which sounded like: "I have come," and as he drew closer I realized I was right, that was what he was shouting. "Jesus has come, I have come." And the entire time he was jogging from one side of the street to the other knocking on the windowpanes he could reach. It was a disturbing sight, religious insanity is disturbing.

The initial reaction was as surprising as it was appropriate: a stool came sailing down at him from a fourth-floor window around halfway along the street. It didn't hit him – nor hopefully was that the intention – but it broke into pieces of course. It was very much a wasted effort, the man only grew louder, perhaps he needed confirmation that what he was doing was of importance.

The next reaction was akin to the first, but less concrete, and not without a touch of comedy. A window flew open and a furious voice screamed: "You're stark raving mad, man!" It was only then that I realized that the man on the street was actually dangerous, that he provoked latent inclinations in some of his fellow men, and I thought: can't some rational person, who has no difficulty walking, go down there and put an end to all this? Quite a few heads had gradually begun to appear out of windows along the street, but down below the madman alone held sway.

I was fascinated, I admit, but as time went on perhaps more so by the entire street scene than by the main character. People had ceased being silent, they laughed and called out to one another over the poor wretch's head. I'd never seen the like of such sudden social interaction, a man in the building next door even called out to me. I could make out only the last word, 'blasphemy', and of course I didn't reply. If he'd said something reasonable, 'emergency room' for example, then who knows, we might have begun to nod whenever we saw each other from then on. But a grown man, old enough to be my long-deceased wife's son, who has nothing more reasonable to say than 'blasphemy', I have no desire to have a nodding acquaintance with, I'm not that lonely yet.

But enough about that. As I said, I was fascinated at this teeming life outside my window, it put me in mind of my childhood – it was probably a better time to be old back then, I think, less lonely, and above all you generally died in a timely fashion – when a man emerged from an entranceway. He looked to be in a hurry and was headed straight for the madman. He grabbed hold of him from behind, spun him around and struck him so hard in the face that the madman staggered sideways and fell over. For a moment there was complete silence in the street, as though everyone were holding their breath. Then there was uproar again, and it was now obvious that the unpleasantness was directed at the assailant. It didn't take long before people began emerging from other entranceways, and while the immediate cause of the entire commotion sat silent and seemingly helpless a few meters away, a heated argument broke out which was impossible to grasp the details of, but it was obvious that the assailant also had his supporters, because two youths suddenly came to blows. Oh, it was a black day for reason.

In the meantime, the madman had got to his feet, and while the youths fought –because of him in all likelihood, but possibly for other reasons – and some others tried to break them up, he backed further and further away, until he reached the closest street corner, at which point he turned and sprinted off. It was a relief. And I'll tell you, that man could run.

When the crowd on the street realized the man was gone, things slowly began to settle down, and one window after the other was closed. I closed mine too, it wasn't a very warm day. The world is full of foolishness and confusion, lack of freedom is deep-rooted, hope for fairness and equality is dwindling, the odds are stacked against us, or so it seems. We should be happy to be doing as well as we are, they say, most people are worse off. Then they take a pill against insomnia. Or depression. Or life. When will a new generation come, one that understands the importance of equality? A generation of gardeners and foresters who can fell the big trees keeping the smaller ones in the shade, and who can remove the suckers from the tree of knowledge.

At the Barber's

I STOPPED GOING to the barber to get my hair cut years ago; the closest one is five blocks away, and in time that became too far to walk, even before the banister on the staircase was broken. But what hair I have I can cut myself, and do, I want to be able to look in the mirror without feeling too depressed. I pluck long nasal hairs too.

But one day, less than a year ago, when, for reasons I won't go into, I was feeling particularly lonely, I landed on the idea of going to get my hair cut, even though it was actually short enough. I did try to talk myself out of it, it's too far to walk, I told myself, you don't have the legs for it, it'll take you at least three quarters of an hour each way. But it was no use. So what if it does? I replied. I've plenty of time, time is the one thing I have too much of.

So I got dressed and went out. I wasn't exaggerating, it took a long time, I've never heard of anyone who walks as slowly as I do, it's a nuisance, I'd rather be a deaf-mute, what's the good in hearing after all? And why speak, who's listening, and is there anything left to say? Well, yes, I suppose there are things left to say, but who's listening?

Eventually I got there. I opened the door and went in. Oh, how the world has changed. Everything inside was different, only the master barber was the same. I greeted him but he didn't recognize me. It was disappointing but of course I didn't let it show. There were no empty seats. Three men were being shaved or having their hair cut, and another four were waiting, and there was nowhere to sit. I was so tired, but no one got up – the ones waiting were too young, they didn't know what it meant to be old. So I turned toward the window and looked out at the street, pretending that was what I actually wanted to do, so no one would feel sorry for me. Politeness I'll accept but you can save sympathy for animals. All too often I've noticed young people – actually, it's been a while since I have, but has the world become more humane? – all too often, I've noticed young people stepping over helpless people lying on the pavement without uttering a word but no sooner do they set eyes on an injured cat or dog than their hearts overflow. *Poor doggy*, they say, or *poor little kitty, have you hurt yourself?* Oh, there are so many animal lovers!

Fortunately, I didn't need to stand for more than five minutes, and it was a relief to sit down. However nobody spoke. In the old days both the wider world and matters closer to home were drawn into the barber's, now there was just silence; I'd walked for nothing, there was no longer any world people wanted to talk about. So after a while I stood up and left. After all, what was the point? My hair was short enough.

And I'd saved some money, probably a fair few kroners. So I walked the several thousand small steps home. Oh, the world is changing, I thought. And silence is spreading. It's time to die.

Thomas

I'M GROWING TERRIBLY OLD. I'll soon find it as difficult to write as I do to walk. It's going slowly as it is. No more than a few sentences a day. And a couple of days ago I passed out. So I'm probably nearing the end. I was working on a chess problem when it happened. I noticed a sudden faintness. It felt like life itself was ebbing away. It wasn't painful. But slightly unpleasant. And then I must have lost consciousness because when I came around my head was on the chessboard. Both kings and pawns lay toppled. It was exactly how I wanted to die. It's probably too much to ask, to die without pain. If I was to fall ill, be in great pain, and sense that the sickness and suffering had come to stay for good, it would be nice to have a friend to help me into the nothingness. That's forbidden by law, of course. Laws are conservative, unfortunately. So even doctors prolong a person's pain, even when they know there's no hope. It's called medical ethics. But no one is laughing. People in pain usually don't. The world shows no mercy. They say that during the great purge in the Soviet Union those who were condemned to death were shot in the back of the head while being returned to their cells to await their punishment. Suddenly, without warning. I think that was a trace of humanity in the midst of all the misery. But there was an outcry among people: they should at least be allowed to die facing a firing squad. Religious humanism is more than a little cynical, well, humanism in general.

Anyway, I came around with my face among the chess pieces. Other than that, it was pretty much like waking up after a normal sleep. I felt slightly confused. I didn't know what else to do but put the chess pieces back into place. But I wasn't able to concentrate on solving the problem. I was just about to go over to sit by the window, when the doorbell rang. I won't answer, I thought. It's probably just some evangelist who wants to have me believe in eternal life. There've been a lot of them lately. Superstition seems to be experiencing a surge in popularity. But then it rang again and I found myself in two minds. They do usually ring only once. So I called out "just a moment" and began making my way to the door. It took a while. There was a boy there. He was selling raffle tickets to support the local school's marching band. The prizes were an unintentional insult to the elderly. A bicycle, backpack, soccer cleats, and the like. But not wanting to appear dismissive, I bought a ticket. Even though I don't care for band music. My wallet was on the dresser so I had to ask him to come inside with me. Otherwise he would have had too long to wait. He walked behind me. He had probably never moved so slowly in his life. Along the way I killed time by asking what kind of instrument he played. "Oh, I don't know," he said. I thought that was a strange answer but I presumed he was shy. I could have been his great-grandfather. Perhaps I was. I do have many great-grandchildren but I don't know any of them. "Are your legs very sore?" he asked. "No, they're just awfully old," I replied. "Ah, okay," he said, seeming reassured. We reached the dresser and I gave him the money. Then I was seized by a bout of sentimentality. I felt he'd had to use an unreasonable amount of time to sell just one ticket. So I bought one more. "That's really not necessary," he said. Just then I suffered a sudden dizzy spell. The room began to spin. I had to hold on to the dresser, and in so doing I dropped the open wallet on the floor. "A chair," I said. As soon as he'd brought it over, the boy began picking up the money lying strewn on the floor. "Thank you, young man," I said. "Not at all," he replied. He placed the wallet on the dresser. Looking at me with a serious expression, he said: "Can't you ever go out?" and it dawned on me that I had probably been outside for the last time. I can't risk passing out on the sidewalk. That would mean the hospital or the old folks' home. "Not anymore," I replied. "Oh," he said, and looked at me in a way that made me feel sentimental again. I've become an old fool. "What's your name?" I asked, and his answer only made matters worse. "Thomas." Obviously I wasn't going to tell him that I had the same name, but it put me in a peculiar, almost solemn frame of mind. Well, perhaps it wasn't so strange. The bell had just tolled for me, as it were. So I suddenly got it into my head that I wanted to give the boy something to remember me by. I know, I know, but I wasn't quite myself. So I asked him to take down the carved owl standing on top of the bookcase. "That's for you,"

I said, "it's even older than I am." "Oh," he said, "I couldn't." "Yes, my boy, yes-yes. And I want to thank you for your help. If you'd be so kind as to make sure you close the door tightly behind you." "Thank you so much." I nodded to him. Then he left. He looked happy. But he might have just been pretending.

Since then I've had several dizzy spells. But I've placed the chairs I have in strategic positions. It makes rather a sorry mess of the room, almost gives the impression of it being almost uninhabited. But I'm still living here. Living and waiting.

archipelago books

is a not-for-profit literary press devoted to
promoting cross-cultural exchange through innovative
classic and contemporary international literature
www.archipelagobooks.org